Cathy, The Girl From Utah

On the cover: Chrysoula, the author's sister. Photography by Constantin Coralis.

This is a work of fiction. The situations and scenes described, other than those of historical events, are all imaginary. With the exception of well-known historical figures, none of the characters portrayed are based on real people, but created from the imagination of the author. Any similarity, therefore, to anyone living or dead, is coincidental.

Library of Congress Card Catalog Number 00-135207

ISBN 0-9660449-1-4

First published in 2001
By Cosmos Publishing Co., Inc.
P.O. Box 2255
River Vale, NJ 07675
Phone: 201-664-3494
Fax: 201-664-3402
E-mail: greekbooks@worldnet.att.net
Web site: greeceinprint.com

Printed in Greece

CONSTANTIN CORALIS

CATHY, THE GIRL FROM UTAH

Translated by Peter Demopoulos

COSMOS PUBLISHING

THE AUTHOR: Constantin Coralis was born in Vissani, a picturesque village of Ipirus Greece. He lived for many years in Brazil where he immigrated in 1953. Before turning to writing, Constantin worked in many other professions. At the age of ten he was a goat herder in the mountains of Ipirus. Later he worked as a waiter, carpenter, musician, opera singer, soccer player, and in many other small trades.

Initially, Constantin started writing poems, short stories, and stories and poems for children, many of which were published in American newspapers and magazines. Some of his poems have been translated into English. In 1997, The National Library of Poetry of the United States included in its beautiful album, *Sunshine and Daydream*, Constantin's poem "America." His beautiful poem "Statue of Liberty" was published in the book *Outstanding Poets of 1998.* These two poems were also published in Greek in the Greek-American daily National Herald of New York. Another of his poems, "Mother Nature," was sent to the White House and President Clinton responded with a congratulatory letter.

However, the most significant work by Constantin Coralis became a reality after many years of labor and is the autobiographical book describing the turbulent and very interesting life of the author. This book was published by Dodoni Publishing Co, November 2000, in Greece with the title *Costantino.* His second book is *Cathy, The Girl From Utah*. Currently, Constantin, is working on his third book, entitled *I Am Haunted by My Past.* As the author correctly observes, "The past is not haunting only me, it is haunting everyone."

Constantin is married and has two children. He now lives in Santa Monica, California.

THE TRANSLATOR: Peter Demopoulos obtained a BS degree from UCLA and a MS degree from Caltech. He has written the Greek subtitles for about a dozen American feature films and translates for the Greek Consulate in Los Angeles. He was the editor of *Yper, The Greek Magazine* published in Los Angeles. Currently, he is the president of the Hellenic Club of Southern California, a Greek cultural organization.

CHAPTER 1

In the middle of June, on a Tuesday afternoon, the Boeing 747 aircraft arriving from London landed smoothly at the San Francisco International Airport. Eventually, the airplane engines quieted down. In preparation for exiting the aircraft, the passengers started getting up from their seats and moving about trying to get the circulation going after sitting for so many hours. Among the passengers were Demetrio Rendis, his wife Dora and their two daughters, three-year-old Annoula and Marianthi, who was one year older.

When they got off the airplane, Demetrio and his family followed the other passengers to the passport checkpoint. Demetrio was carrying two small suitcases and kept looking at the huge crowd around him while Dora walked alongside holding her two young daughters tightly by the hand. When they came before the immigration officer, Demetrio placed the passports on the counter.

"Demetrio Rendis," mumbled the airport immigration officer without lifting his eyes from the passports in front of him. "You are coming from Athens through London. Is that right?"

"Yes, sir," answered Demetrio immediately with a smile.

The immigration officer lifted his eyes and looked at them quizzically. "You are Greeks?"

"Yes," replied Dora, who knew a little more English than her husband. "But we have Argentine citizenship."

"Do you realize that your Visa permits you to remain in this country for 10 days only?"

"Yes, we know this very well. We are just passing through," Dora replied, blushing faintly.

An hour later Demetrio and his family had made it through customs and were on a second flight to Los Angeles. Demetrio was restless. "I am not sure, Dora, maybe we should continue south to Argentina. We can re-establish our swimsuit business there."

"Demetrio, do you forget how bad things are there with inflation?" Dora replied. "Crime is getting worse. Every day everything gets worse. Remember Samuel?"

"The Jewish fellow?"

"Yes, the Jewish fellow. Remember how those men entered his store, robbed, and killed him? These things happen all the time now. America is a big place. There are opportunities for everyone. You are a hard worker, and I will help you. Think about our children."

"Our children . . ." Demetrio whispered. He turned and drew his wife to him tightly. "I love you all," he said softly. "I love you more than my own life."

When they arrived in Los Angeles, it was already dark. Christo, Demetrio's uncle, was waiting for them. He was a large man, 60 years old, and a building contractor by profession. He had lived in the United States for 30 years. Christo had married while still a young man, just after arriving in the US. He had two sons and a daughter. Now, he was divorced. His 18-year-old daughter and 20-year-old son lived with their mother in San Diego, two hours south of Los Angeles. His oldest son, who had turned 22 that year, lived with his girl friend in Phoenix, Arizona.

"Welcome!" Christo thundered as he stretched his large arms to embrace Demetrio and Dora. Then he leaned down and kissed Marianthi, and then immediately grabbed little Annoula and lifted her up. "Hey, you pisser," he bellowed joyfully as he spun her around. "Do you still wet your bed?" The child blushed and shook her head vigorously, winding her arms around her uncle's massive neck.

The group walked to the baggage claim, retrieved the family's luggage, then found Christo's station wagon in the parking lot. They loaded it up and drove directly to his house in Culver City, a suburb of Los Angeles, just 20 minutes away.

As Christo turned the car into Sepulveda Boulevard he threw a glance at Demetrio. "I see, nephew, you are thinking hard. What's bothering you?" he asked.

"Ah, nothing, uncle. I am just a little tired from the trip."

"I don't want you to worry about anything, young man. Job and housing are no problem for you. I own more than 60 apartment units, which require a lot of maintenance. You'll always have a Mexican helper with you. And don't worry about staying in America after your visa expires, we'll take care of that, too."

Demetrio listened to his uncle's words, but his mind wandered from Buenos Aires to his native Greece. Demetrio had always been a dashing man. When he served as a Commando in the Greek army some of his fellow soldiers nicknamed him "Giant." He was always among the first and the best in military exercises, and he always marched in the front row of parades, towering above everyone else.

After completing his two-year obligatory military service, Demetrio returned home to Konitsa, a beautiful village in the prefecture of Ioannina in Northern Greece, near the Albanian border. But life there quickly became dull. Demetrio spent long hours helping his father run the cafe under the huge sycamore trees in the townsquare.

It didn't take him long to realize that Konitsa was too confining, and when he could no longer bear it, he decided to follow in the footsteps of so many other restless Greeks and immigrated to Argentina with one of his friends.

Life in a foreign land was difficult, and Demetrio soon began to regret his decision. He desperately wished to return home, but couldn't face the embarrassment of having to admit he had made a mistake. For five long years he stayed in Argentina, before returning home to his family and his birthplace. In Konitsa, he found his mother seriously ill. His sister Eleni had married a nice young man, Dionisis, who worked as a wood-shop instructor at the village orphanage school just a short walk from the townsquare.

Demetrio's father tried in vain to convince his son to stay home and take over the family coffee shop. "Stay home, Demetrio," he would say sadly. "Don't go away to foreign lands when you can make a decent living right here. We'll find a nice girl for you so we can have all our family together. I don't want to die one day without you near me."

"Yes, Dad. I'll return one day, I promise. Just give me a little more time. I'm just getting established there. I started up a little shop making swimsuits. Everything looks very promising and I'm sure I will succeed. Besides, you are not alone here. You have Eleni and Dionisi, and Mother is getting better. In a few more months, you'll have your first grandson." The father hugged his son tightly. "Son –, " he began, but his voice broke and tears rolled down his cheeks.

It was April and everyone was busy preparing for Easter, the most important holiday of the year. On Holy Thursday, Eleni baked tsourekia, the traditional Easter bread, and dyed eggs the deep red color of Christ's blood, following a custom that stretched back for centuries. Demetrio stayed to share the holy days with his family. Early that morning, he went to hang out with his childhood friends in his father's cafe. When he returned home shortly before noon, he found his mother almost half-asleep, sitting on the straw swing chair on the wooden deck of the verandah. He kneeled and kissed her.

"How are you, Momma? I see you are getting better," he said.

"Yes, son. When you are here, all of us feel better."

Suddenly, she kissed her son's hands softly, and he felt her warm tears.

"Please, Momma, don't cry," he said. "I am not going to war. As soon as I organize my shop a little better and make some money, I'll be back. I don't want you to think I like living down there by myself." Then he rose and stroked her hair lightly while trying to appear happy. "Is Eleni inside, Momma?" he asked.

"Yes, son. She is inside. Dora is here, too."

"Dora? Which Dora?"

"Katero's daughter."

"Oh, yes. I remember her, we were in the same school," he said casually.

Demetrio went inside and greeted his sister and her friend. "Hello, girls," he said with a smile. He went up to his sister and laid his hand on her stomach. "How's the baby?" he asked.

"Everything is fine, Demetrio, except I have to wait two more months for the stork to come." Then she turned to face him. "Do your remember Dora?"

"Sure I remember. How are you, Dora?" he asked the young woman sitting next to Eleni. "How are your parents? Is everyone well?"

"Yes, I am fine, everyone is fine," she said stretching out her hand to shake his. "And how are you? It's been a long time."

"Exactly five years," said Eleni, giving her brother a big hug.

After a while, Dora left. "Tell me, little brother," Eleni

asked, "how are you doing with the girls in Buenos Aires? Do you have a girlfriend?"

"No, nothing really serious. I've had a few little adventures, but no one special."

Eleni took his arm and pulled him towards the verandah. "Demetrio, I want to talk to you."

"What do you want to tell me? Is something wrong?"

Eleni laughed. "I just want to talk to you about Dora."

"Dora?"

"Yes, Dora. Don't you want me to talk to her? She is a very nice girl. Besides, she's been crazy about you from the moment she laid eyes on you."

"To tell you the truth, sister, I like her, too," he said with a big laugh.

"Why are you laughing?" asked Eleni.

"Because I remember Dora when she was a kid in school. How skinny she was. We used to call her 'The Board'. Now I look at her and wonder how she got to be so beautiful."

"Well, what do you say?"

"What can I say? I like her, but we have to ask her about this."

"Don't you worry about that. I have already talked to her. I'll invite her to have dinner with us tomorrow. This will give you a chance to get to know each other better."

A few days before his departure for Argentina, Demetrio and his father went to Dora's house to make an official proposal of marriage. "I'll return to marry your daughter, Mr. Thomas, as soon as I can," Demetrio promised after Dora's father had given his consent. "I give you my word of honor."

"Call me father, my son. It will be an honor to have you as my son-in-law." Then he turned to Demetrio's father. "Costa," he said, "let me hug you, too. I'm just so happy. Dora, bring some ouzo to celebrate this happy event!" The glasses clinked as everyone wished Demetrio and Dora a long and happy future.

A few days later, Demetrio left for his long trip back to Argentina, but his mind remained in his beloved Konitsa with Dora, who had completely captivated him. When he had asked her if she would join him in Argentina after their wedding, she had looked at him steadily and had said, simply, "I will always be with you."

As soon as he arrived in Buenos Aires, he began immediately looking for a nice house to buy. He wanted very much to please Dora when she arrived. He finally found one in Belgrano, not far from his job. It was in a pretty and quiet middle-class neighborhood. Demetrio began dreaming of having a family and children. He loved children.

All through that summer, Demetrio wrote frequently to his parents and Dora. In December, he returned home for the holidays, and for his wedding. Then he and Dora flew back to Argentina. Within a few months, Dora had gained a good grasp of Spanish and could talk easily with the women who worked in his shop. She even helped increase their production. In the evenings, the two of them would sit together in the living room watching television and making plans to return home to their families. The next October, their first daughter was born. Dora would frequently hug her husband. "I am so happy, Demetrio. I owe everything to you. A year ago, I didn't know what happiness meant."

Demetrio would smile, lift her up, and spin her around. "I love you too, Dora. I love you very much. Let's be patient for a little while longer. Soon, we'll all go back to our Konitsa, once and for all."

In early April, Demetrio made arrangements to fly home for Easter so their daughter could finally meet her grandparents, and so they could personally deliver the news that Dora was two months pregnant. The holiday, however, turned out to be an unhappy one for Demetrio. His mother became very sick and died within a few days of his arrival. Fortunately, his father lived with Eleni who took good care of him and offered him some solace in his time of deep sadness.

Back in Buenos Aires, Demetrio grew silent and pained. “Dora,” he said one day, “I’m thinking we should be going back home. We’ve spent too many years far away from our families. I don’t want our children to grow up in a foreign land. We have suffered enough.”

Dora never disagreed with her husband’s decisions, and she, too, was homesick. In November, their second daughter was born, and shortly after that, they sold their home and business and returned to Konitsa for good.

Back home, everyone was happy. Dora and Demetrio deposited their savings in the National Bank of Greece and were able to live comfortably on the interest. But, within a few months, Demetrio once again grew restless. Hanging around the cafe helping his father seemed to him a silly way for a grown man to spend his days. He was used to living in a big city like Buenos Aires and now everything in Konitsa seemed too small and confining. “Dora, we should have stayed a few more years in Buenos Aires,” he would say. “At least until the children are old enough to start school.”

“Darling, don’t worry so much. Everything is going to be all right. What’s important is that we are all together now.”

When Demetrio’s father died a year later from a stroke, Demetrio could no longer stay in Konitsa. He could no longer abide the place. Earlier that year, his uncle Christo had invited him to bring his family to America. Without thinking it out clearly, Demetrio decided to accept his uncle’s invitation. That’s how he ended up in Los Angeles on that Tuesday in June.

CHAPTER 2

The days passed and still Demetrio had no clear idea why he had come to America. In Argentina, at least, he had felt comfortable. The Argentines were more outgoing and seemed so much happier than the Americans, and their language was easier. After eight months in Los Angeles, Demetrio still had difficulty understanding when people spoke to him. Slowly, his loneliness and the monotony of his life began to wear on him. He longed for the fresh air and sunshine of Konitsa and for his friends and family. He longed to break free from the grueling work routine that left little time for other things. Time slipped steadily away from him, each day as uneventful as the last, and Demetrio grew increasingly depressed. Dora also suffered, but silently. She tried hard to hide her pain and justified their life by thinking of the advantages they were gaining for their daughters.

"We are doing all this so our children can have a better future," she reminded Demetrio. "What would our children do in Konitsa? Where would they go to school?"

"We could have moved to Ioannina," Demetrio protested. "Did we have to come to the other side of the world so the children can go to school? This is no life here."

"Don't forget, Demetrio, the promises Uncle Christo made to us. He has in his will one apartment building for each child.

Our kids will have some financial comfort when they grow up."

"So what? It's just promises" murmured Demetrio half to himself.

Demetrio grew very concerned about the environment in which his children were growing up. Every day, when he dropped Annoula and Marianthi off at school, he saw kids idling about, behaving badly, and this depressed him. He heard stories from his friends that worried him. One was about a 16-year-old girl who ran away from home leaving behind a note telling her parents not to worry. She promised to call in a few days to let them know where she was. Her grandmother, who loved her dearly, had a heart attack when she heard of the news and died in the back of the ambulance as it rushed to the hospital. Her father tried desperately to find her. He hired private detectives, knocked on doors of government agencies, all to no avail. After eight months, the girl returned home asking for her family's forgiveness. Two months later, she gave birth to a daughter.

Fortunately, Annoula and Marianthi were enjoying themselves in their new home. They soon made some new friends. Near Christo's house lived a Greek family with three children, who were a little older than Demitrio's daughters. In the afternoons, the kids took their bikes and skateboards and went over to the alley between the two neighboring homes. Marianthi had already learned to ride a bike and Annoula ran happily behind her holding her little doll which she always carried. Uncle Christo often took the kids to Disneyland, Universal Studios, and other magical places.

Demetrio took charge of all the maintenance work for his uncle's many apartment buildings. He drove a small Toyota truck his uncle had bought for him and usually worked with an illegal immigrant from Mexico, or another Latin American country. Demetrio's assistant at that time was a Mexican named

Renato. Renato was a jack-of-all-trades, skilled in carpentry, plumbing, painting, plastering, and electrical work. His wife and three children lived with his parents in Oaxaca, Mexico. Renato had come to California five years earlier, hoping to earn enough money to feed his family. He had followed in the footsteps of thousands of other Mexicans searching, he would say, for the American dream. Renato's plan was to work hard, save enough money to return to Mexico, and buy a small farm. However, it didn't take him long to realize that in America he could earn no more than minimum wage, a wage that made it difficult to survive. When work was plentiful, he could earn enough to send some back to his family. From the stories Renato told, and the photographs he showed, Demetrio got the impression that Renato and his family lived in extreme poverty.

But, instead of solving his problems, Renato multiplied them. While far from his family, Renato met Blanca, a young woman from El Salvador who was separated from her husband and who had a two-year-old son, Rodrigo. Blanca was looking for a man to support her and provide a home for her and her child. Renato needed a woman. All he needed was a woman, but soon they started living together and, after three years, they had two more children of their own.

When Renato first told his story, Demetrio was incredulous. Later, he realized that Renato's situation was not all that uncommon, and that it was one that could very easily get worse. One day, Renato came to work so beat up Demetrio had a hard time recognizing him. One of his eyes was black and swollen shut, and his face and neck were covered with bandages. "Renato, what happened?" Demetrio asked.

Renato smiled as best as he could. Holding his chin in the palm of his hand he said, "Blanca's husband Eduardo showed up last night and wanted to take her back. We had a fight." Suddenly, his face contorted and his one good eye turned black with anger. "Next time he shows up," Renato vowed, "I will kill him."

Not too long after that, Renato didn't show up for work for several days. Demetrio went to his apartment to find him. There, he met Blanca for the first time. She was crying. She explained to Demetrio that Eduardo had come back a second time and Renato had stabbed him with a butcher knife. He died in the hospital the next day. Renato fled, and the police were searching for him. Demetrio began to realize how very different this world was from the one he had left in Konitsa.

A few days later, Demetrio was lying on the couch watching television when he heard a light knock on the door. It was late, and Dora and the kids were sleeping. Christo had gone to Las Vegas for the weekend. "Who could it be at this late hour?" Demetrio mumbled as he went to the door. "Who is there? " Demetrio asked.

"Demetrio, it is me, Renato! I need to talk to you." Surprised, Demetrio opened the door. Renato stood there, looking disheveled and scared. Demetrio moved aside to let him in. Renato took a few steps and immediately began pleading with his friend. "Demetrio, I need help. You are the only one who can help me. For five days I have been sleeping in the bushes under freeway bridges. I took no bath, I stink, and I am very hungry."

Demetrio looked at him with sympathy and asked, "Is it true that you killed Blanca's husband?"

"Yes, but first he tried to kill me. I did it in self-defense. The knife was his. He was holding it out when he showed up at the door. While we were struggling, I knifed him. Now the police are looking for me. I must leave for Mexico right away."

"Will they let you through at the border?" Demetrio asked.

Renato smiled. "That's not the problem. The problem is that I don't have any money at all." Then he said, "Demetrio, forgive me for coming here to disturb you. You are the only friend I have."

Demetrio worried that he might find himself in trouble if the police came looking for Renato in his home. But his conscience would not allow him to turn Renato away in this condition. Demetrio grabbed Renato by the arm. "Renato, the first thing you need is a hot bath. Let's start with that and then we'll figure out the rest. Try to be very quiet because everyone is asleep." Before sending Renato to the bathroom, Demetrio grabbed a big black trash bag from the kitchen and handed it to him. "Throw all your clothes in here. I'll give you some of my clothes to wear."

After a long hot bath, Renato pulled on Demetrio's clothes and walked to the kitchen where Demetrio had set some food on the table. As Renato ate, Demetrio asked, "What are you going to do now?"

"I'll go over the border and I'll try to make it back to my village. The danger will be over once I get there."

"What about your children here? How is Blanca going to make it with three kids and no one to help support them?"

"I think about that all the time. But what can I do? I am still afraid to go near the house because the police are probably watching for me there. God will take care of them. At least here in America the government helps out. The children were born here and have their rights. It's not like Mexico where the stinking politicians have completely abandoned the poor people to their fate."

As soon as Renato finished eating, Demetrio showed him to the sofa for the night. Early the next morning, before Dora woke up, Demetrio drove him south past San Diego. They stopped when they came within sight of the Mexican border. When they got out of the car, Demetrio handed Renato $ 300. Renato was moved by his friend's generosity. They hugged each other and Renato, his voice faltering, said, "You are a good man, Demetrio my friend. I will never forget you."

"I wish I had more to give you," Demetrio replied.

The two men shook hands again and Renato turned and headed towards the border. Demetrio stood there, watching. Just before Renato disappeared from view, he turned and waved one last time. Demetrio returned the salutation. "Good luck to you, Renato," he whispered.

On his drive home, Demetrio thought about how much Renato's life had changed in just a few days, and about how complicated life can be and how much suffering goes on in the world.

On Monday, when Christo returned from Las Vegas, Demetrio recounted Renato's story. Christo became upset. "Did you forget that you are here illegally, too, and you could have been arrested and deported? Because of you we can all get into a lot of trouble for harboring a criminal. If you get a police record you will have a big problem staying here. They will never give you the green card. You can even go to jail. I can get into trouble, too, because of you, and they'll be pulling me around like a rubber band. The police here don't fool around, you know. It's not like Argentina, my friend, where you can always bribe somebody. The law here is tough and it is enforced. Even if they catch you pissing in the street, it's a crime and you can pay dearly. Here, nobody can do what he wishes, you know. Didn't you think what could happen to your children?"

Demetrio listened silently to his uncle's harangue. He did not wish to show his uncle disrespect by arguing.

A few days after Renato left, Demetrio found another assistant, a Nicaraguan named Raul. Demetrio picked him up one morning from the sidewalk where dozens of illegal immigrants congregated every morning hoping to be found by someone needing cheap laborers. It didn't take Demetrio long to realize that his new helper had a problem with liquor.

Raul often came to work half-drunk. One morning, when Demetrio and Raul were replacing a window in a second floor apartment, Raul almost lost his footing. Some days he would arrive with the smell of wine heavy on his breath, barely able to stand on his feet. "Raul, how come you stink of wine so early in the morning?" Demetrio asked.

"No, Demetrio, it's not wine. I only had two beers, " Raul protested, throwing his arm around Demetrio's shoulder. "Serveza, amigo Demetrio. Solamente serveza, no vino."

When Demetrio found out that Raoul had five young children and a sick wife, instead of firing him, he decided to try to help him. He convinced Raoul to go to Alcoholics Anonymous for treatment. Christo was supportive of this. To give moral support, Demetrio often accompanied Raoul to his AA meetings where he had an opportunity to see a different side of the world. There he saw what it meant to be a derelict, and realized the devastation that alcoholism brings to society and the terrible struggle it takes to recover from the claws of this disease. Many fail because they cannot overcome the hold that the disease has over them. But it didn't take long for Raoul to radically improve. He started coming steadily to work, clean-shaven and wearing clean clothes. Christo agreed to Demetrio's request to give Raoul a good pay raise, something that made Raoul extremely happy.

"Uncle, do you realize that it's already eight months since Raoul joined AA and he still goes there?' Demetrio asked one day.

"Demetrio, it seems that he is a success. One more life was saved. Let's hope that Raoul doesn't fall again into the trap of alcoholism."

CHAPTER 3

One day, Demetrio woke up with an ear infection and decided to see a doctor. When he arrived at the office, the nurse ushered him into a small room with a glass door. He sat down and put on a set of earphones. The examiner adjusted the buttons and asked him to raise his hand when he heard a sound. When Demetrio came out of the booth a few minutes later and asked if everything was all right with his ears, the nurse replied, "The doctor will explain it all to you."

The doctor came in and told Demetrio that he needed to see a specialist for more tests. "I suspect that something is going on with your right eardrum and, if you don't take care of it, you might lose your hearing," he said.

"But doctor, I've never had a problem with my hearing in all my life. I can hear a pin drop."

The doctor insisted that Demetrio visit the specialist. Otherwise, he warned, he could not be held responsible if something were to go wrong with Demetrios's hearing. Demetrio walked out of the office and went to the front desk. The receptionist handed him a bill for $ 400. The hearing specialist's business card was attached. Instead of following the doctor's advice, Demetrio went home to Dora. For the next few days, she inserted two warm drops of olive oil in his ear, following her mother's traditional remedy. Soon, Demetrios's pain disappeared.

Demetrio's uncle had had a similar experience with doctors. Once, he had gone skiing in Canada with some friends, and came down with a terrible cold. When he returned home, he went to see his doctor. The doctor prescribed some antibiotics and instructed him to return as soon as they were used up. Because Christo was very concerned with his health, he closely followed all of the doctor's instructions and returned as soon as the prescription was gone. After examining Christo again, the doctor said, "I suggest that you have the X-rays because there are some unusual sounds in your breathing and I don't like it."

"Doctor, I don't feel that bad. I want you to know that every day I run five miles without stopping. If I had something in my lungs, I wouldn't be able to run like that."

The doctor put his hand on Christo's shoulder and said, "As your doctor, and also as your friend, I want the best for you. We are doing all these tests to prevent something worse."

Even though Christo had known this doctor for many years and had a lot of confidence in him, he ignored the doctor's advice and went to another, who, after examining him, said, "Friend, if all patients were as healthy as you, I would soon be out of business."

Despite his age, Christo was still a ladies man. Frequently he would take one of his girl friends and travel to Las Vegas for a weekend. During holidays, he would stay even longer.

When Demetrio returned from work one day he found his uncle watching television in the living room. "How are you, Uncle?" he asked.

"Come and sit next to me, Demetrio. Tell me, how was your day today?"

"Everything was fine, Uncle. Fortunately, Raoul is very good nowadays and he doesn't drink any more."

Christo laughed. "What would I have done without you, nephew? You were a godsend. Demetrio, tomorrow is Friday. I am planning to go to Las Vegas and come back on Monday. Do you want to come with me?"

"Me come with you, uncle?"

"Yes, you will get the chance to see Las Vegas, the dream-city. It is not right that you have been here so many years and you still haven't seen the place."

"Uncle, I'd love to come but I don't want to leave Dora and the kids here by themselves."

Christo thought for a moment. "You are right. Then we go one day early in the morning and come back that same evening."

"Uncle, how is that possible? Just to go there takes more than five hours, plus five to come back."

Christo looked at him and smiled slyly. "Demetrio, it only takes a half hour to fly. Dora will not even realize we are gone. We don't have to tell her, it's not a big sin!"

Christo and Demetrio planned to leave the following Monday. The night before their departure, Demetrio told Dora that he and Christo had a big roofing job scheduled that would keep them away all day. Dora never doubted her husband. She simply asked him to be careful working on the rooftop.

The next morning, Demetrio said good-bye to his family. He and Christo jumped in the truck and in a few minutes they were at the airport and on their way to Las Vegas. But Demetrio's excitement was tempered by pangs of guilt. He had never before lied to Dora. As the plane was touching down at the Las Vegas airport, Demetrio turned and confided in his uncle. "Dora is such a wonderful woman, uncle, that I feel real bad doing this. She doesn't deserve this," he said.

"Come on, Demetrio, don't feel so bad. You will like it

here so much that you'll forget all about your guilt. You will especially love the beautiful girls here."

"Girls? What girls?"

"You'll see," his uncle replied.

From the airport they took a taxi which delivered them in front of a huge casino. As they entered the casino, Demetrio looked around him in amazement at its size and glitter. "Uncle, what is all this. Is it real? This casino is as big as a city."

"You haven't seen anything yet. Wait until you see the rooms upstairs. There is nothing more luxurious in the whole world." Christo knew Las Vegas well because he visited the city and all its casinos frequently. "Come on, Nephew, what do you want to play?" he asked.

Demetrio saw the huge crowds moving about the casino, playing the tables and slot machines, and he wondered where they all came from. It was only ten in the morning. "Uncle, what time do they open up this place?" he asked.

"Demetrio, all Las Vegas casinos stay open 24 hours every day of the year. They never close!" Christo led Demetrio to the cashier where he bought two buckets full of coins and handed one to Demetrio. "Here, take these," he said smiling. "Now, Nephew, come let us try our luck. Watch me and do as I do." Christo sat in front of a slot machine and started to feed it with coins. Every time Christo deposited a coin in the machine's voracious mouth, he pulled a lever on the right side and the coin magically disappeared.

Demetrio imitated his uncle. The rhythmic sound of the levers and jangling of the falling coins reminded him of the strange drumming of wild tribes engaged in ritual celebrations. In a few minutes, all the coins in Demetrios's bucket were gone.

"Uncle, how much do the coins cost?"

"One dollar each."

"A dollar? How much have we lost so far?"

"Two hundred," Christo replied shrugging his shoulders indifferently.

"Two hundred? Let's get out of here, Uncle. We will lose our pants in here!"

"Don't worry, Nephew," Christo said and poured another handful of coins into Demetrio's bucket. "We came here to have fun."

When they lost those tokens coins as well, they moved to a blackjack table. Within a few minutes, both men had lost quite a bit of money there, too. Demetrio looked at his uncle, incredulous at how willing he was to throw his money away.

At noon, they left the casino for the restaurant. After they were seated, Demetrio asked, "Uncle, have you ever won any money here?"

"Demetrio, people don't come here to make money, they come here to have fun. If they win money, so much the better."

After lunch, Demetrio and Christo returned to the casino. "Demetrio, wait for me here," Christo said. "I'll be back in a little while." Then he disappeared into the crowd.

Alone, Demetrio looked about him feeling lost. "People come here to have fun losing their money!" he thought. Demetrio leaned against a huge column, and waited until he heard his uncle's voice behind him.

"Demetrio, let's go," Christo said.

"Where are we going now, Uncle?"

"Let me show you the hotel." They walked to the elevators and ascended to the 7th floor. When Christo unlocked the door to their room, Demetrio was once again amazed at the luxury.

Christo picked up the phone and spoke to someone for a few seconds. "Now, nephew, lie down and rest for a while. In the afternoon, we'll be leaving."

"You rest, Uncle. I am not really tired. I'll watch some TV."

About a half-hour later, someone knocked at the door. "Demetrio, go see who it is," Christo commanded.

When Demetrio opened the door, he found two beautiful women in their twenties. "Hi!" they both said in unison.

"Hi!" replied Demetrio. Before he could say anything else, the two women moved past him into the room.

"Hello, girls!" Christo said with a big smile.

One of them went up to Christo and kissed him softly.

" This is my friend, Lola," she said, pointing to the other young woman standing in the middle of the room.

"Hi, Lola!" said Christo. "Let me introduce to you my friend Demetrio."

Lola sauntered up to Demetrio and put her arms around his neck.

Demetrio could not believe what was happening. Christo, sensing his nephew's discomfort, said, "Nephew, how do you like the surprise I have for you? Do you like Lola?"

"Uncle, I don't know what to say. The surprise is interesting, and Lola is beautiful."

" Look, Demetrio, Judy and I are going over to the next room. You and Lola can do whatever you want. You can go down to the main casino and have a drink. My wallet is on top of the dresser. Take a couple of hundred dollars and gamble it." Christo turned and left with Judy, closing the door behind them.

Lola wound her arms around Demetrio's neck and kissed him. "Demetrio," she asked softly, "do you like me?"

Demetrio stood there, momentarily awkward and passive. "You are beautiful!" he finally blurted out. She grabbed him tighter and kissed him on the lips passionately. This time Demetrio could not resist and returned her passionate kisses. "You are beautiful, Lola. Yes, you are very beautiful." He lifted her up and carried her to bed.

"You are a strong man, Demetrio, you have big muscles. Where are you from?"

"I am from Greece. I've been in America a few years now. I am married. I have two children and I love my wife."

Lying on the bed, Lola said to him, "Come to me. I don't want to break up your marriage."

Demetrio thought he detected an accent in Lola's speech, and asked where she was from.

"I am from Brazil, Demetrio," she replied.

"I have heard a lot about Brazilian women but I have never known one before."

"It's never too late. You have a Brazilian girl in front of you now. You can have me and eat me."

Demetrio laughed. "I don't think I could eat you."

Lola stretched out her hands. "Come and try, and if you like me, you can eat me. A girl friend told me that Greeks are hot men, like the Italians. But I have never met a Greek before who could verify this."

"Tell me Lola, have you been many years in America?"

"No. I've only been here a year. A friend and I came as visitors, to see Las Vegas, and we decided to stay a while longer."

"Did you stay because you like Vegas or for the money?"

"No, it's not that. Actually, my parents are well off. They have coffee farms near Sao Paulo. I am an only child. My father thinks I am still touring the USA and keeps sending me money."

"I don't understand. If you don't need the money, why are you doing this?"

"I love my job," she responded immediately. "I must be the daughter of Aphrodite. My dream is to write a book about my experiences with men, though I must admit, I have not yet met the man of my dreams."

Demetrio laughed.

"Why are you laughing, Demetrio? Don't you believe me?"

"No, no. It's not that. I am just thinking what kind of men you must meet."

"Yes, you are right. Most of my customers are usually older. You see, it's hard for a younger man to come here when it costs $ 500 a visit."

"What!" exclaimed Demetrio. "Five hundred? I don't have that kind of money with me!"

"Don't worry, darling. We have been already paid by your friend. It's our policy to always get paid in advance."

"That man is not just a friend, he is my uncle. I work two weeks to make five hundred," Demetrio whispered shoking his head in amazement.

Lola had slowly slipped off her clothes and was lying stretched out on the large bed wearing only her underwear. Demetrio took in her well-proportioned body and perfect breasts. Lying against her warm body, Demetrio lost track of time. Eventually, he got up and went to knock on the door of the adjacent room. There was no response. "Lola, we must go now," Demetrio said. "I've got to get back home tonight."

"Demetrio, let me tell you another secret. My real name is Vanda. Now tell me, do you want to take a shower with me? It'll be quicker."

"Let's go, let's go, he said laughing."

"You know something, Demetrio, one of these days I'll jump on a plane and go back to my country. I'm starting to get bored with this kind of life."

After they dressed, they ran to the elevator and Demetrio impatiently pounded on the call button. When the elevator arrived and they were inside, Vanda opened her small purse, pulled out her calling card, and handed it to Demetrio. "Keep it," she said. "Next time you come to Vegas call me and I'll entertain you in my home. I am staying in a little apartment of my own."

When they got off the elevator, she took his arm in hers. Touching her lips to his ear she whispered, "You are a powerful lover and I like it. It's a shame you live so far away. Remember me when you visit Las Vegas next time, I will treat you as a special guest, free of charge."

"Thank you, Vanda, but I don't think I can come again. My world is very different from yours."

"Demetrio, if you want I can come to Los Angeles to see you.

My friend, Judy, has your uncle's phone number. I'll call him and leave a message for you. Okay?"

"Oh, no, no. That's impossible. I told you I am married."

Lola leaned close to him. "Demetrio, darling, when I write my book you are going to be the main character, the hero. I already have the title of my book. It's called 'The Loves of Lola.' But now I think I am going to change the title. I'm going to call it 'Demetrio the Greek.' What do you think? Do you like it?"

"Yeah, yeah. It sounds good, but tomorrow, when you meet an Italian, you might change the title again. Demetrio will become Giovani."

"Oh, no, my love. I have met many Italians, most of them younger than you. But you are at the top. You are head and shoulders above every one of them."

As they turned the corner, Demetrio spotted Christo gambling at the blackjack table. He walked up to him and asked, "What time are we leaving?"

"Tell me, what time is it?"

"It's 5:15 Uncle."

"Okay. In ten minutes we are leaving. Walk around with her for a few more minutes and then come back."

"Vanda, you should probably be leaving now, don't you think?" Demetrio asked.

"Sure, I am leaving. But first let's go and play the slot machines until your Uncle is finished." Later, she confided that she never gambled. "All my friends, Demetrio, lose their money to these one-armed bandits. That's why they have nothing. I save my money. This year I have saved over $ 100,000"

Startled, Demetrio asked, " "Vanda, are you serious? One hundred thousand? That's a lot of money."

"Yes, Demetrio, it is true. I have some customers who give me as much as $ 3,000 for a tip. That's in addition to the regular fee which they pay at the office."

"What office are you talking about?"

"The customers don't negotiate directly with us. When a man or a woman wants an escort, they call the office. Ask your uncle, he knows everything about that."

Demetrio laughed. "You mean there are also male escorts?"

"Sure. Who do you think escorts the ladies, especially the somewhat older ones? I am surprised, Demetrio, that this is so strange to you. Where have you been?"

A little later, Demetrio walked Vanda to her car. She turned and hugged him. "I am not leaving unless you promise me that you'll come again."

"Yes, I promise. I'll come to see you again," said Demetrio as he pulled her hands gently from his neck.

When Demetrio returned to the casino, Christo asked, "Where have been, Nephew? I've been looking all over for you."

"I see you are happy, Uncle."

"Yes. I am happy, nephew, because I think you brought me good luck. Whenever I come to Las Vegas alone, I always lose. Today, I won more than what we spent and I have an extra thousand left over. Since we are partners in this, half of it belongs to you."

"Oh, no, Uncle. That's yours. I don't want anything."

"Come on, come on, take it now and watch not to say anything around the house because we will both be ruined. Dora will kill me for spoiling you."

"Don't worry, Uncle, I will keep my mouth zipped about this."

On the way to the airport, Christo asked Demetrio if he had enjoyed their trip.

"Uncle, you know I like it, but I feel so guilty about Dora. I hate to cause her any pain. I think I made a big mistake coming here."

"Now, come on, Demetrio, that's nonsense. Stop saying it's a mistake. It was just a little adventure, a diversion from the routine. Nothing else!"

Around 7:30 that evening, they arrived home. Dora opened the door, greeted her husband, hugged and kissed him. "You worked very late today. You must be very tired," she said.

"I'm okay, Dora." Demetrio replied. "Don't worry."

"Well, I can imagine how tired you must be today. Now go and take a hot bath while I serve dinner."

"Yes, it was a long day," Christo said, "but at least we got the job done."

After his return from Las Vegas, Demetrio was a changed man. He had always been kind to Dora, but now he tried to compensate for his misdeeds and to assuage his pangs of guilt. He settled again into his routine, and time moved as predictably as the hands on the wall clock making their rounds. Christo, on the other hand, kept disappearing every weekend, sometimes driving south to San Diego or east to Las Vegas.

CHAPTER 4

A few days before Christmas, Demetrio and his family went shopping at the local mall. Suddenly, they heard loud voices and saw people running in all directions. Demetrio grabbed Marianthi and Annoula and pulled them close. Dora looked about fearfully. Soon they realized that a four-year-old boy had disappeared. His desperate parents, the police, and nearby shoppers were trying to find him. Demetrio had heard of child kidnappings on the news and from his friends, but he had never been this close to one. As he watched the boy's mother and heard her screaming, Demetrio felt her panic as if it were his own. "Carlito, hijo mio" she cried. "My God, I want to die, I don't want to live without my son. Carlito! Carlito!"

For a while, Demetrio stayed among the circle of curious onlookers who had gathered at the scene. Then he guided his family into a store where they quickly bought a few presents for the kids. Then they walked hurriedly to their car. Demetrio drove silently, brooding over the incident at the mall. Every so often, Dora would make the sign of the cross, praying, "Holy Mother of God, keep us safe, keep us from evil."

After the holidays, Demetrio tried once again to convince Dora to return to Greece. Months before, she had been adamantly against the idea, but now she agreed to go. Demetrio approached his uncle with their decision. Christo was very upset and tried to convince him to change his mind. "Demetrio, are you sure you want to abandon the good future that's ahead for your children? What does Greece offer that you don't have here? You should think more about the future of your young ones."

"Yes, Uncle, my kids are what concerns me the most," replied Demetrio. "It's for them that I want to go back. I think this world here is too big and moving too fast for us. Uncle, do you know how I feel? I feel like a kid who loves candy and suddenly finds himself in a candy store filled with chocolates, cakes, and bonbons, and he can't decide what to buy. Finally, he settles on an enticing piece of cake, but it turns out be nothing beneath its pretty wrapping. Then he realizes that everything in the store is fake – they are just for show. That's how I feel in this huge wealthy country."

"Demetrio, I don't think it's quite as bad as you say. All these people who come to America, they make out well financially."

Demetrio laughed. "I've been working with you now for four years but if I tell you how much money I have saved, you will laugh."

"Well, you shouldn't have bought that brand new car for Dora. You know what people say about money? It's hard to earn, easy to spend."

"But Uncle, Dora needs the car to take the kids to school. I tried two times to make it with used cars. I spent a fortune fixing them and there were times she needed to go places but the car didn't work."

"Yes, Nephew, but the school isn't that far. They could have taken the bus."

"Uncle, you don't understand. The kids are in danger when they are out on their own."

"Listen, Demetrio, I have promised that I will leave in my will one apartment building for each of your children. But this can only happen if you stay with me, just like I was here till the last moment when my own uncle passed away."

"Uncle, we didn't come to America because you are rich. We came here to work. I brought my family here because I believed I would find a better life, and not because I expected you to give apartment buildings to my kids. We never imagined this when we left to come here. Uncle, we don't like it here, therefore we will go back even if we are offered all the millions in the world to stay."

Suddenly, Christo rose from the couch. "Ungrateful people!" he shouted. "You are all ungrateful. That's what you are. Christo was very angry now and paced the living room with his hands behind his back, his eyes staring at the floor. Then, suddenly, he stopped and sat down.

Demetrio was quiet for a few moments. Then he said, "Uncle, it upsets me very much when you talk to me this way. You shouldn't think like that. We love you because you are part of our family and not because you can give us property. Believe me, Uncle, we expect nothing from you. Whatever we have now in the bank in Greece is adequate for our needs. I want to make it clear that we did not come to America to take your property."

Christo was silent. Suddenly, he turned to face Demetrio. "Nephew, I apologize. I know that you are a proud man and a good person. You are not the type to take advantage of anyone." Christo leoned forward and gave his neplew a hug. "Demetrio, I want to tell you something that's happening to me. Please, try to understand. The years are passing and I panic when I think I may be alone when I get older. When you came here I felt much different. Having you near me, a young man, I feel good, I feel secure. I enjoy seeing your kids here, too. They make me forget my age. That's why, when you talk about returning to Greece, my legs break from under me. I feel terrible about my own future when I'll be alone." Tears began to roll down Christo's cheeks.

"For God's sake, Uncle, don't feel like that. You should know that we will always love you. Don't panic like that and things will be all right."

The next morning, when Demetrio recounted to Dora the discussion he had with his uncle, she listened carefully and then said, "I don't know what to say, Demetrio. I feel very sorry for Uncle. It's very tough for him to live alone."

After much encouragement by Demetrio, Dora and the children returned to Konitsa to spend their summer vacation. "Stay as long as you want," Demetrio said as he waved them off at the airport. "All that fresh air and sunshine will be good for you and the kids. We'll manage all right here."

Only after Demetrio returned home did he realize how empty and silent the house was without Dora and the kids. Each night, when he returned from work, with no one there to greet him, he felt terribly depressed and lonely. He tried to soften his loneliness by calling Dora frequently.

One night, Demetrio was watching television with Christo when his uncle turned to him and said, "Demetrio, I am inclined to sell everything and return back to Greece. The only reason I have stayed here till now is my children. But I realize they don't really care for me. When I go to San Diego to visit them, they are not interested in me. Sometimes they are not home when I arrive, even though they know I am coming. Their mother, nephew, has filled them with hatred for me. She has turned them against me as though I am their enemy. My oldest son, Nicholas, moved to Phoenix without letting me know about it. I don't even know his address."

"I feel for you, Uncle," Demetrio answered.

"Demetrio, I was, and still am, a good father. I cannot understand my children's indifference. But now it is time to move on, sell all my properties, and go back to Konitsa. It will take some time. Things are complicated, Nephew. I have my wife involved, too, because our divorce is not final yet. She wants all my property even though none of it belongs to her. I inherited it after our separation. And yet we are still in and out of courts."

"What can I say, Uncle? If you decide to go back, it will be easier for us to return also. I don't believe we are better off here than we would be back home."

The summer months passed slowly, until, finally, the time came for Dora and the kids to return home. Demetrio immediately felt better.

One Monday night, when Christo returned from Las Vegas, he found Demetrio watching TV in the living room.

"Are you alone, Demetrio?" he asked.

"Yes, Uncle. The kids are in bed. Dora went to bed about a half-hour ago. What's new? Tell me, how was your trip?"

"Demetrio, do you remember the girl I was with when we went to Las Vegas together?"

"Sure, I remember her."

"What I wanted to tell you is that her Brazilian friend is crazy about you. She didn't call you because she didn't want your wife to find out. Judy told me that she wants desperately to see you again."

"Uncle, this is impossible. I thought I had explained everything to her. I don't want adventures or to break up my family."

"Demetrio, calm down. I understand that, but it's not necessary to break up your family over this. Don't over-react. I am a lot older than you are and I know something about life. A little adventure now and then is good for you. Even if you are happily married, it does you good because it gets you out of the rut, especially if it is with someone like that Brazilian girl... what's her name?"

"Vanda is her name."

"As I was saying, what man can refuse to have a little adventure with Vanda?"

Christo got up from the couch and patted Demetrio on the back. "Now I'm going to take a quick bath and I'm going straight to bed. Tomorrow, we'll talk again about this. Good night, Demetrio."

"Good night, Uncle."

That night, Demetrio had trouble falling asleep. His mind kept turning to Vanda, no matter how hard he tried to think of other things in an effort to forget her. He thought of her smile, her laughter as she stretched out on top of the king-size bed, beckoning him to come to her. His thoughts brought a sweet shiver through his body that traveled from his feet and terminated in his brain. At that moment, he felt such a strong desire for Vanda that he forgot everything else in the world. When his surge of desire had subsided, he glanced at Dora and silently apologized for his weakness. He despised himself for allowing his passions to torture him.

The following year, toward the end of spring, Dora received word from her father that her mother was seriously ill. As soon as school was out, she and the children left for Konitsa. Soon after, Christo mentioned that he was going to Las Vegas to look over a property that was for sale. Demetrio jumped at the chance to go with him. During the flight to Las Vegas, Demetrio could think only of Vanda.

They arrived in Las Vegas Airport at 11 a.m. Demetrio immediately found a phone booth and called Vanda. Her voice on the answering machine said, "This is Lola. Please leave your name and phone number and I'll call you back as soon as possible."

Demetrio felt his body tingle. "Vanda, it is me, Demetrio. I am here in Las Vegas with my uncle. I will wait for you at the Blue Sky Casino," he responded.

When they met that afternoon, Vanda looked as beautiful as he had remembered.

"Today you are really pretty," Demetrio said, pulling her close to him.

"Thank you, Demetrio. I want to be pretty only for you," she said smiling. "You are not going to show me your room?"

In a few minutes, they were alone. Demetrio lifted her and carried her to the bed. "Vanda, I want you very much," he whispered holding her around her waist. Demetrio loved to hold her waist. Vanda kissed him all over his body and fondled him sweetly. Later, when they took a shower together, Demetrio could not stop admiring her beautiful body.

"Vanda, you have the most beautiful breasts I have ever seen," he said as he bent down to kiss her nipples." Her body responded, and she lost herself in her pleasure. When Demetrio told her he would remain in Las Vegas for a few days, she jumped with joy.

"And your wife?" she asked.

"She took the kids and went to Greece for a couple of months," Demetrio replied. Vanda flung her arms around his neck and covered his face with kisses.

"We will stay at my home together for as long as you are here. I'll take you to the best shows in town. If you want, we can even go down to Brazil for a few days. This will give you a chance to meet my family and you'll get to know my beautiful country. What do you say, Demetrio? Come on, say yes!" Without answering, he pulled her close to him and she rested her head against his chest. "I love you, Demetrio. I love you so much."

"I love you too, my little Vanda. But our paths in life lead in different directions. I think fate has it for us to have met at the wrong time." Holding her, Demetrio felt guilty and confused. He loved Dora, and he could not understand why he could not control his passion for a woman he had met only once before. He tried to convince himself that his actions were insignificant, nothing but physical passion, a natural phenomenon that makes the attraction between a man and a woman irresistible.

During the time that Demetrio was in Vegas, Vanda took time off from work so they could spend time together. Demetrio and Vanda attended many of the shows, and surprisingly many of them were free.

Demetrio, being a simple man, saw all this and could not believe it was real. He thought he was in a world of fantasy. Something else that impressed Demetrio was the food. Every hotel has its own special cuisine.

"Vanda, I am sure that all Vegas hotels and casinos lose money on food and drinks. How is it possible to dine on New York strip steak with salad and baked potato for only $ 6? And at the buffets, you can eat all you want for $ 3? I don't think there is cheaper food anywhere else in the entire country."

Vanda explained to him that the food was used as an enticement to get people into the casinos, where they spent the real money.

Before coming to Las Vegas, Demetrio had heard many horror stories about the casinos and gambling. Now he had the opportunity to see for himself. Vanda told him about an Arab gambler, who was also one of her customers. In a short time, the man had lost $ 680,000 playing baccarat. A Chinese gambler lost so much money on cards and the roulette that he committed suicide in his hotel room.

"You know what I am thinking Demetrio," Vanda said. "Deep down all gamblers must believe that they will lose all their money, but they do not want to think about it. It is an amazing sight to see people from all walks of life – rich, middle class, and probably many poor – happily gambling their money away. Las Vegas has discovered the secret of getting people to gladly hand their money to the big casinos. The propaganda machine has been perfected to the point where just about everyone believes Las Vegas and gambling is good, fun entertainment. Now, they even have family attractions so that children are sucked in. You can see how good business is, Demetrio, as they continue to build large and luxurious casinos that employ thousands of people. No wonder Las Vegas is the fastest growing city in the United States."

Demetrio felt happy being with Vanda, but as the days passed, he grew uneasy. He felt their initial anemic bond growing stronger, and he worried where it might lead. Eventually, his uncle concluded the negotiations for his real estate purchase, and it was time for them to leave. Demetrio realized that his fairy tale existence was coming to an end.

The day before they had planned to leave Las Vegas, Demetrio and Vanda decided to spend a day at Lake Mead, 30 miles away. To Demetrio, Lake Mead looked like an immense, calm sea with an amazing view and jagged shoreline. This was the first time Demetrio had ever seen such a large man-made lake. They rented a boat and went fishing, releasing their catch back into the water. In the afternoon, they visited the marina and boarded the Desert Princess, a triple-decker paddle wheeler for a spectacular 90-minute cruise over the clean, blue waters of the lake. During the cruise, Demetrio heard a tour guide tell the story of the construction of Hoover Dam and Lake Mead. Work for this gigantic project started in 1931, and more than 5,000 workers labored on it for five years. More than nine million tourists, from all parts of the world, came to camp, boat and fish there each year. To Demetrio, everything looked beautiful that day. The sky was blue and the temperature pleasant. Demetrio felt content. He could not remember ever being so relaxed and carefree. Even his family was far from his thoughts.

During the ride back to Vegas, Vanda said, "Demetrio, I would be the happiest woman if I could spend my whole life with you."

"Vanda, you know that's impossible. From the first moment we met I told you the story of my life. I never hid anything from you."

"Yes, I know it. But that doesn't stop me from dreaming. When I think that one day I will return to my country and I will not see you again... my mind stops.... Ah! I forgot to tell you. My father visited me last month. He insists I go back. He is such a good father. He never refuses anything. 'I am not going to send any more money,' he told me, trying to be tough on me. Yet, when he left he gave me $ 5,000."

When they arrived back at Vanda's apartment, Demetrio said, "Vanda, everything about today was beautiful, but now sit close to me as I want to talk to you seriously. You are a young and very attractive woman. You should go back to your country to find a young man and have a family together. It's a beautiful thing to have your own family." Vanda was curled up in his arms, and he felt her body shaking. "Baby, are you crying? Why are you crying? I don't want to see you like this. I love to see you laugh. When you are happy and playful with me, that's how I like you."

"Demetrio," she said without pulling loose from his arms. Please, don't advise me to marry somebody else because I feel that you don't want me. I don't want anybody else. I only love you. I promise, I will never cry again. I will try to be always happy to make you happy. I love you, Demetrio, and I want you. You know what I have been thinking lately? I have made up my mind never to marry. I am not a little girl anymore not to know any better. I thought very carefully and concluded that there is no word 'marriage' in my dictionary. Most women nowadays get married to have someone to take care of them. Personally, I don't have this need. My problem is something different." She stopped and looked at him. "I love children. The only thing I want in life is a child. Demetrio, I want to have a child with you. Please, give me a child."

Demetrio was astonished.

"Don't worry, Demetrio. I will never be a burden to you. Besides, I'll go back to Brazil and you will be here in America, or maybe even in Greece. What do you say? Don't you want to give me a baby?"

Demetrio took her in his arms again. "Do you want a little boy or a little girl?"

"Does this mean you agree?"

"Yes, Vanda. If you want it so desperately, I cannot deny it."

"Demetrio, hold me tight, my love. I love it when you hold me tight in your arms. I feel your power passing through my body. I am in love with you Demetrio. Now I want to tell you something else. I quit my escort job. You know why? I don't want another man to touch my body ever again."

Then she looked at him. "You believe me, don't you?"

"Certainly I believe you. I think you did the best thing you could have done. Now you must devote all your time to our child."

"Demetrio, you have no idea how happy I am. Oh, I didn't tell you. I bought a Greek-English dictionary. Now I know how to say in Greek 'Love', 'sky', 'sun', 'moon', and some other words. When I go back to Sao Paulo I'll go to school to learn Greek. I must teach our child the language of his father."

Suddenly she paused. "There is something I never thought of before," she said.

"What is? Let me hear it."

"Our child will be asking about his father. I must think of a story to tell him. But I have plenty of time to think of a good one. Let's hope that precious moment arrives, and then we'll see."

Demetrio was listening to her carefully. His face had taken on a strange expression and his eyes were far away. "These are not easy things, my little Vanda. Just imagine me knowing that I have a child living far from me, so far that I can never hold him. You know, we Greeks love our families very deeply, we adore our children with a pathological desire. No, Vanda, I don't want you to have my child. We will all suffer if this happens."

"You should not be thinking this way, Demetrio. I will do everything possible for our child to be happy. Besides, our child is going to be neither the first nor the last to live without a father. What's important is that we can give life to a new human being, and this we do with pure love. From the moment I met you, Demetrio, I saw what every girl dreams about —true love. A serious man, measured in all respects, strong, and desirable. I am very upset because we met in the sickening environment I was in. Forgive me, Demetrio." Then she started to cry.

Demetrio held her and silently stroked her beautiful hair.

Later, Demetrio called his uncle to ask him what time they were to meet for the airport in the morning. "Demetrio, I can't leave tomorrow," Christo said. "We have to make the final inspection of the property. There are some minor repairs that still need to be done. Do you mind if you stay a few more days?"

Demetrio was ecstatic with this unexpected turn of events. "No, Uncle. I don't have any problem at all. I can stay here as long as you need." When he set down the phone, he started yelling, "Vanda... where are you, baby?"

She ran out of the kitchen. "What happened, Demetrio?"

When she came to him, he lifted her up, spun her around and said, "Baby, I am not leaving tomorrow. I'll stay here a few more days with you."

During the days Demetrio spent in Las Vegas, Vanda was

constantly with him. She even helped with the repairs on the property. Every afternoon, she would go home to prepare a new and delightful Brazilian dish for their lunch. Demetrio discovered that he loved black beans with long-grain rice, and chicken with potatoes and vegetables. Demetrio realized that Vanda was a good housekeeper, an excellent cook, and always in good spirits. Every afternoon at about 4:00 she would come to pick him up from work. At home, everything was ready and in top shape. The table was set, the clothes nicely folded, and dinner on the table. She had a pleasant singing voice, too. Oftentimes, while playing Brazilian music on the stereo, she would sit on his lap and sing. At times, she tried to explain the meaning of the lyrics to him. Demetrio most enjoyed the work of the great Brazilian composer and singer Roberto Carlos. One of his favorites was:

"How many times I thought of returning back to you
To tell you that my love for you has not changed at all
But my silence was more powerful
So that every day I'm dying away from you
And you do not know it..."

Demetrio was in no hurry to complete his assignment in Las Vegas. Every time his uncle called to check on the progress, Demetrio would say that he had discovered yet another problem that caused more delays.

"Demetrio, it seems that you will soon abandon us for your Brazilian girl," Christos told him one day with a smile.

"What are you talking about, Uncle? Me? Abandon my family? Never! You know me better than that. I would never do that." At the thought of his family, Demetrio felt very guilty. Nevertheless, he tried to put his guilty feelings aside with the excuse that his Las Vegas escapades were temporary and soon would be forgotten.

Having stretched his stay by several days, Demetrio finally

decided to leave Vegas and return home. The time was approaching for Dora to return from Greece. Vanda was depressed as she drove him to the airport.

"My little Vanda, I cannot stand seeing you like this! You have to be strong and keep me strong, too. I am suffering with our situation also," Demetrio said.

Vanda drove silently, keeping her eyes on the road. Once in a while, she would take his hand and hold it tightly.

When they said good–bye, she fell in his arms crying.

"I love you, Demetrio, I love you so much."

CHAPTER 5

As the plane turned towards Los Angeles, Demetrio gazed out the window and started to think that Vanda's desire to have his child was rather odd. Although he felt flattered, he had second thoughts and the idea no longer appealed to him.

In the beginning of September, Dora returned from Greece bringing with her the sad news that after several months of suffering, her mother had passed away leaving behind Dora's father, who was now all alone. Dora worried about him and wanted to return to Greece.

"My father can't live by himself at his age," she told Demetrio. "He needs someone to take care of him. I can't abandon him now."

When Demetrio, one more time, brought up the idea of going back to Greece, Christo was very much against it. "You want to go back now, Demetrio? Now that I just bought another building? Maybe it would be okay in a few years, but not now. My suggestion is to bring Dora's father here. That way he will be close to all of us." This idea seemed very reasonable to both Demetrio and Dora. When she told her father, he agreed, too. The next day, Christo went to see his attorney about filing the paper work needed to bring Dora's father to the United States. But there was a problem. Neither Demetrio nor Dora were U.S. citizens, so they couldn't serve as her father's sponsor. Neither could Christo, who was not related to him. Without a sponsor,

Dora's father could not immigrate. After holding a family council to determine what to do, they decided to keep things as they were and have Dora travel to Greece at least once a year with Christo footing the cost of the tickets. Dora was satisfied with this arrangement, and so was Demetrio.

That Christmas, Dora departed for her annual visit. A few days after her departure, Demetrio asked his uncle if they could take a quick trip to Las Vegas. Christo laughed. "You missed that Brazilian girl, you rascal! I don't blame you though. She is real cute. But watch out not to fall for her and forget all of us."

"What kind of talk is that, Uncle? Don't let such an idea cross your mind."

"I understand, Demetrio. What you are doing is just to satisfy the flesh. Isn't that so?"

Demetrio smiled. "That's all it is, Uncle."

For most of the time that Dora was in Greece, Demetrio was in Las Vegas with Vanda. She was still very much in love with him, but she was anxious.

"Demetrio, why our baby is not coming? Could it be that I can't have children? Maybe I should go have a doctor examine me. What do you think? Should I go now or wait some more?" Then she cuddled and whispered in his ear. "You have to visit me more often so we can spend more time together. Don't you think I am right?"

"Yes, Vanda. I'll try to visit you more often."

Every now and then, Demetrio would call Dora on the phone and talk with her and the kids. To prevent any embarrassment, Demetrio had made an arrangement with Dora. Using the excuse that calling from Greece is much more expensive, he told her that he would initiate all calls. This suited Demetrio because this way Dora could not find out if Demetrio was ever away from home. In this deception, Demetrio had the full cooperation of Christo.

The days passed quickly. Christo came from Los Angeles to be with them for the holidays since he had no one else. This gave Christo the opportunity to get to know Vanda a little better and he started to like her. "She is a good girl, Demetrio. But still, she is a street walker." Demetrio didn't pay much attention to what Christo was saying.

On January 4th, Demetrios returned to Los Angeles, and two days later Dora arrived from Greece. Then something strange began to happen to Demetrio. The depression that had plagued him for years began to lift. He no longer felt guilty about the double life he was leading. He knew he would never leave his family and, more significantly, Vanda's presence pleased him and made him happy. Work no longer bored him. He enjoyed it, and started singing again just like in the old times.

Even Dora noticed the change. "What else can I do, Dora?" Demetrio asked. "I am beginning to come to terms with our situation. I think of the problems other people have, sometimes not even having enough food, and I realize how fortunate we are."

Christo was very cooperative in the cover-up. Whenever Demetrio wanted to go to Vegas, he would ask Christo to help out by providing a good excuse. Dora would nod with a pleasant smile. "Don't worry, Uncle. If he has to go do something useful, then he must. He is not going there for fun."

Demetrio would leave early in the morning on the first flight out. He would call Vanda just before boarding so she could come to the Vegas airport to pick him up. Upon meeting him, she'd fall in his arms and stay there for a long time. She'd laugh and cry while gently stroking his hair, kissing him, and cradling his head in both her hands. "Demetrio, I love you. I always thank God for sending you to me. I appreciate your coming to visit me."

"I love you too, Vanda. And I want you. You have no idea

how much I want you. But as I told you before, we met at the wrong time in our lives." For Demetrio, Vanda was the cure for his depression because he was no longer bored. She was always waiting with open arms to receive him and give him all the pleasures his heart desired.

While talking with Christo one day, Demetrio brought up the subject of the baby that Vanda wanted to have with him. "Oh, Demetrio, you put so much faith in what women say," his uncle replied. "Do you believe what a whore says? They just tell you what you want to hear."

Offended, Demetrio countered, "Please, Uncle, don't condemn all women. Vanda is not a whore. She did whatever she did because she was young and easily influenced. I wish you knew how good she is. Believe me, she is a very giving person with a good character."

Christo was not convinced. "Whatever you tell me about her, Demetrio, I don't believe it. If I were in your place, I'd have all the fun I could get from her but try to stay away from this kind of woman."

Demetrio changed the subject because he didn't want to argue with his uncle who, after all, was his only ally. Christo called even his ex-wife a "whore," the mother of his own children. According to Christo, the only woman who was not a whore was his own mother.

One Friday afternoon, as Demetrio was working, Christo came to see him. "Uncle, what brings you here?" Demetrio asked.

"I have brought a message from your lover. She wants to speak to you right away. She said it's urgent." Then Christo pulled the cellular phone from the pocket of his leather jacket and handed it to Demetrio. "You can call her right now," Christo said and walked away to give him some privacy.

"Vanda, my love, how are you, darling?" Demetrio asked when she picked up the phone.

"I have to see you right away, Demetrio. If you can't come, I'll take a plane for Los Angeles I've got to see you."

"Vanda, you know I can't see you here. Let me talk with my uncle so I can make arrangements and I'll call you right back."

"Okay, I'll wait. Do whatever you can, but come."

Demetrio hung up and went over to Christo. "Uncle, it's some kind of an emergency. I have to go to Vegas. I need your help. Find some kind of an excuse for Dora. Tell her there was an emergency repair job. Tell her part of the roof fell down and I had to take care of it. Or whatever you can think that's more appropriate. I need at least a week."

"Don't worry Demetrio. I'll take care of Dora. I'll tell her the roof leaked very badly during yesterday's rain and it ruined all the upstairs apartments."

"Thank you, Uncle, for your understanding."

Christo did what he could to encourage Demetrio's relationship with Vanda because as long as he was involved with her, he would postpone all thoughts of returning to Greece.

Demetrio called Vanda back. "Honey, I'll be there tomorrow at 10:00. Wait for me at the airport."

"Yes, darling. Thank you for coming."

At dinner that evening, Christo brought up the matter of the leaky roof in Las Vegas and emphasized that it was an emergency. "Demetrio must go right away to take care of it," he told Dora.

Early the next morning, Demetrio threw some clothes in his suitcase, said good-bye to Dora and left with Christo who was driving him to the airport. When he arrived in Las Vegas, Vanda was waiting. Right away he sensed something was wrong. When he held her hands, they felt cold and clammy. "Vanda, darling, what's wrong?" he asked.

She hugged him tightly for a moment without speaking.

Then she said, "Let's go, Demetrio. We'll talk about it at home." When they reached the car, she handed him the car keys. "Demetrio, please, you drive."

"Okay, but tell me what's the problem?" Demetrio asked as they drove away from the airport parking lot.

"I have some bad news and some good news, but let's wait until we get home. With some patience everything can be taken care of." For the remainder of the ride home, Vanda made small talk, telling Demetrio about the letters she received from her parents, her loneliness when he was not with her, and how happy she was with him sitting beside her.

Later, as they sat on the living room couch in her apartment, she snuggled close to him. "Let's start with the good news. I think I am pregnant," she said bringing his hands to her lips and kissing them.

"Did you see a doctor?" Demetrio asked.

"No, I didn't yet, but I feel strange things happening to my body. My period is 11 days late and my appetite is huge. I can eat anything put in front of me." Then she took his hand and placed it on her breasts. "Do you feel how hard they are?"

Demetrio smiled. "You may be right. But still I think you should see a doctor before drawing definite conclusions."

"Yes, I agree but I want you to be there with me. Tomorrow is Sunday. Can you stay a few days here? Monday we'll see the doctor and, if I am pregnant, next Saturday I'll fly home to Brazil."

"What?" Demetrio shouted in surprise. "What's the hurry?"

"Now I'll tell you the bad news. They keep calling me every day from where I used to work. They want me back. They threaten me. They say an accident will happen to me. I told them I am engaged and I want to quit, but they don't care. They gave me till next Sunday. If I don't go back to work, I have to leave Las Vegas."

"Who are these people? Tell me who they are. Who keeps calling you?" Demetrio's face turned red. "Oh, you dirty bastards, criminals, gangsters," he blurted out.

"Calm down, Demetrio. Calm down my love. The callers don't leave a name. They just leave a message. Nobody can touch these guys because nobody knows who they are. When I went to the office where my old employers are, they laughed when I told them about the calls. 'Somebody is teasing you, lady. Nobody can force you to work if you don't want it yourself. We live in America, not Russia.' However, the guy saying these things had a strange expression. His laugh was strange and cold. As I was walking out, he was sizing me up from head to toe. I felt his eyes following me all the way to my car. I am not afraid for me, Demetrio, only for our baby. Our baby has the right to live and grow up." She broke into tears.

"I really got you into a lot of trouble, my baby Vanda," Demetrio said. She didn't say anything but remained in his arms gripping his hands desperately. He kissed her gently. "Don't worry my love, I will always be with you to protect you. Monday we are going to the doctor and then we decide what to do."

"Demetrio, I have reserved a flight going directly to Sao Paulo. No matter what, I've got to leave this city."

When they went to the obstetrician on Monday, Vanda's suspicions proved true. "You definitely have a baby there. Congratulations," the doctor said. They walked out of the doctor's office holding each other tightly. "How I want to be with you, Vanda, now that you need somebody to help you," Demetrio said.

"Don't worry about me, Demetrio. Don't forget that I'll be with my parents who really adore me and will give me a lot of support. I'm going to miss you though so very much, but I expected this from the very beginning. Be assured that I am psychologically prepared."

Before going home, they stopped at a small restaurant on Las Vegas Boulevard for a bite to eat. "You must eat well now," Demetrio said placing his palm on her stomach. "Our baby boy has to be healthy."

"I am sure, he will be strong just like his father. But we don't know if it's a boy or a girl," replied Vanda smiling.

"That's how I like you. Smiling and happy. I want to always remember you with a happy face," Demetrio said.

Suddenly, Vanda became very serious. "Demetrio, when do you think we'll see each other again?" He did not reply. "Can't you say something?"

"What can I say? I don't know what to say. I don't know what to think. Let's change the subject. I don't like to think about this at all."

The days passed quickly. On Saturday morning, they sat at the kitchen table for breakfast. They were silent and gloomy. Demetrio pulled a small leather bag from his pocket and placed it in Vanda's palm. "It's a small present for our baby," he said.

She opened it up and found a beautiful gold cross hanging from a thick gold chain. She brought it to her lips and kissed it. "Thank you my love, thank you very much," she said. Then she got up, stood behind his chair and wrapped her arms around him, touching his face lovingly with hers.

Before leaving the apartment, Demetrio asked for a sheet of paper and started writing. When he finished, he folded it. "I wrote my name: Demetrios Rendis. Write it on the baby's birth certificate. Also, if it is a boy, and if you don't mind, register him as Costa, my father's name."

"Certainly, I will name him Costa. But how are we to name her if she is a girl?"

"DEMETRA!" Demetrio said with a wide smile.

Vanda sat down, wrote something, and handed him the piece of paper. "It's my address. If one day you feel like seeing us, you can come, anytime. As for me, I swear to God and on the cross you gave me for our baby, I will always wait for you till the end of my life. I belong only to you, my love. All I ask is that when I die, I want to be in you arms." Tears rolled down her eyes. Demetrio kneeled next to her.

"My little Vanda! Don't cry, please don't cry. God will take care of all of us and we will find the right path in our life."

A little later, Demetrio was driving Vanda to the airport, unable to sort out his thoughts. Only after he had parked the car did he realize that Vanda was leaving him forever. Earlier, when he had asked her what to do with the car, she had pulled the title from her purse and had signed it over to him. "Keep it, or sell it if you don't need it. It's a small gift from me to you."

"Vanda, this car is practically brand new. I can't take this as a gift. I'll try to sell it and send the money to you in Brazil."

She smiled. "Please, don't send me anything. If I needed money, I would have sold it already. Promise me, you'll keep it?" Demetrio nodded without saying a word. "Now come close to me. I want to kiss you. Hug me, Demetrio. Hold me tight in your arms for the last time, my love. Hold me as tight as you can." Vanda was crying, her body shaking in Demetrio's arms.

Demetrio could no longer hold back his tears. Unable to find the right words to express his emotions, he remained speechless. He searched for something comforting to say to Vanda, but in vain. They just stood there, crying in each other's arms.

CHAPTER 6

Demetrio remained at the airport until he's airplane took off and disappeared into the horizon, leaving only a ribbon of black smoke behind it. He realized at that moment that a part of him was traveling with Vanda. He lifted his arm to wave good- bye. At that moment he felt pangs of extreme loneliness, as though he had been abandoned in the middle of the great wide desert. But then he remembered Dora and his children back home. Before heading back to Los Angeles, he bought a cup of coffee at the airport cafeteria to calm his nerves. The five-hour drive back was torture for him. Vanda's face was indelibly impressed in his mind. When he finally reached Culver City late that afternoon, he left Vanda's car in a garage and took a taxi home.

With Vanda gone, Demetrio returned to his usual life, a monotonous routine of work, home, dinner, sleep, and work again. He felt as if the terrible tedium were slowly killing him. Dora noticed her husband's unhappiness. "Demetrio, darling, you work too hard," she told him. "You look so sad all the time, slow down a bit."

Demetrio tried to hide his distraction and to resume a satisfying relationship with his wife, but his thoughts were always traveling south to Brazil. He could not believe that he would never be with Vanda again. He tried to imagine Vanda holding their baby. He worried that her parents might cause difficulties for her. His thoughts kept him in constant turmoil, and sadness weighed heavily on his heart.

Fortunately, Vanda did not have any problems back home, and her parents were very supportive. Vanda told them that Demetrio was married, and that she had known this from the beginning. Her parents accepted the situation. "Dearest daughter, you came back and brought us happiness again," said her father. "We want you to be close to us. I am so happy that soon I will be a grandfather."

Vanda prepared for the baby's arrival by shopping with her mother for everything they needed for the nursery. Silvio, Vanda's father, was a muscular man of average height, good-natured, who always had a smile on his face. When Vanda returned, he hired a crew to paint the house, inside and out. He vacated the central bedroom, and prepared it for Vanda. He ordered new drapes and furniture. "My little girl. I see that you are sad and that upsets me. I understand your pain and I want to stand by you and help you, but I don't know how."

"Oh, Daddy, I never expected so much understanding from you. Believe me, I am so very happy and appreciate all you do for me. I am only sad because I think of Demetrio who is not here. Daddy, I love Demetrio with all my heart. What makes me so depressed is the idea that we will always live apart from each other. But I am still satisfied with my life and I always thank God for bringing Demetrio into my life. Do you understand what I'm saying, Daddy?"

"Yes, my little girl, I understand you. I promise you, I will always do my best to make sure you are happy."

Vanda was under the constant care of one of the best obstetricians of Sao Paulo, in one of the best hospitals of the city. Time was passing, her stomach was growing, and Vanda was now counting the days. One day, as she was sunning herself on a chaise lounge by the pool, her father called her to the phone. "Little Darling, come quickly, the call is for you."

Vanda's heart fluttered with excitement. She grabbed the phone with trembling hands and said, "Hello?"

"Darling, how are you?" It was Demetrio.

Vanda's heart skipped a beat. "Demetrio," she began, before breaking into uncontrollable sobs. Her father, was standing next to her.

"Calm down my little sweetheart," he said softly holding her tightly. "Is it Demetrio?"

When she nodded, he took the phone before she even had the chance to respond.

"Hello, Demetrio. I am Vanda's father. My name is Silvio da Silva. How are you, son?"

"I am fine, Mr. da Silva. How is everything there?"

"Here everything is fine. Don't worry about Vanda, we watch her better than our own eyes. Do you understand my English?"

"Yes, I understand you. Besides, my English is no better than yours. I am very pleased, Mr. da Silva, that I have the chance to talk to you and hope that some day we will meet face to face."

"Yes, God willing, my son. And remember, Demetrio: You are always welcome in our home. You can come any time."

"Thank you, Mr. da Silva, thank you very much."

At that moment, Demetrio's nagging doubts melted away. He now felt sure that Vanda and the baby were in good hands, with a family that loved them. He was also encouraged by the sincerity of Mr. da Silva's invitation to call whenever he felt the need.

One week later, Demetrio called again and asked Vanda if she had tested for the baby's sex.

Vanda laughed. "No, Demetrio, I didn't test for that. I'll

surprise you when the baby is born. I love surprises. In fact we are preparing for either a boy or a girl. The clothes we are buying are neither blue nor pink, and can be worn by either a boy or a girl."

Vanda's mother, Margarita, was ecstatic to have her daughter home again. She ordered the gardener to plant flowers throughout the garden. She also ordered four small almond trees to be planted, one at each of the four corners of the yard. This was a gift for her daughter who, as a schoolgirl, had loved to paint mountains covered with flowering trees. Near the pool, they set up a swing for the baby. All was set for the baby's arrival.

Vanda's father began to stay home instead of going everyday to his coffee plantation. Silvio owned 4,000 acres on the outskirts of Sao Paulo. In this fertile farmland, rows of luscious coffee plants stretched over the rolling hills and valleys, while cattle and horses grazed peacefully in the pastures. A small crystal river cut across the land, flowing into a natural lake. Thanks to the abundance of water and nutrients in the soil, vegetable gardens and fruit trees thrived, dotting the countryside.

Silvio employed 45 farm hands, who lived on the property with their families and tended the horses, cows, pigs, ducks and chickens. They made cheese and butter and collected a large number of eggs that they sent to the supermarkets in the suburbs surrounding Sao Paulo. During harvest time, Silvio hired 200 additional temporary workers.

One of the first things Silvio did when his plantation began to prosper was to build a one-room schoolhouse on the grounds for his workers' children. The nearest municipal school was one hour away, a distance too great for them to travel. Silvio hired a teacher from town who came every weekday morning and left in the afternoon. He paid the teacher's salary, and for all the books and writing materials. This way the children on his farm received a basic education that most other children in Brazil lacked.

Silvio's plantation and farm were under the strict supervision of Mourilo, a giant man, who was strong like a bull, honest and faithful to the point where he would sacrifice his life for Silvio. He was one of the first to be hired at a time when Silvio was working at the coffee plantation from daybreak till dusk, and sleeping in the farmhouse together with the other workers. Mourilo had his own horse, which he rode when making his daily rounds.

Silvio and Mourilo became very good friends from the start, so much so that when Mourilo got married, Silvio stood as his best man and later became the godfather of his three children. After Vanda was born, Mourilo and his wife Marinita, a good-natured peasant woman, became her godparents.

The happiest day for Vanda, Silvio and Margarita came on the 17th of September, when Vanda gave birth to a healthy boy. Vanda could not contain her joy.

"Daddy, How I wish Demetrio was here with us in this happiest of days. I miss him so much!" Then she began to cry.

"Don't cry my little darling. These days are happy for all of us, don't cry, honey," Silvio said, his own eyes blurring with tears. At one moment, he asked her, "Do you want me to go to America and bring Demetrio here? I promise that I'll do it, as long as it makes you happy."

Vanda took her father's hand into hers. "Thank you, Daddy, but please don't worry for me because these days I am so excited. That's all. Yes, I want Demetrio to be here but I know it's not possible." Then the nurse brought the baby in. When Vanda took the baby in her arms, she felt an immense love for her child. Her mind wandered far, to Las Vegas, and she imagined Demetrio looking lovingly into her eyes. Gently, she ran her fingers over the baby's head, caressing his fine, silky hair. "My little baby," she said. "You are the steel link that binds me to your father forever."

As soon as she returned home from the hospital, Vanda waited anxiously for Demetrio to call. A few days later, while Vanda was resting in bed and the baby was sleeping in his crib, the phone rang and she lifted the receiver. "Hello!"

"Vanda, it's me, Demetrio."

"Our baby boy was born, sweetheart," replied Vanda.

Demetrio was speechless.

"Demetrio, can you hear me?"

"Yes, darling. How is the baby? Are you all right? Was everything okay with the hospital?"

"Yes, everything was fine. The only problem I have is that I miss you. Do you think you can come visit us?"

"I can't promise you. I want to very much but it is very difficult for me, you know that."

"Why don't you come for a few days when your wife leaves for Greece? What do you think about that? Is that possible?"

"I don't think it's impossible."

As soon as Demetrio hung up the phone, he began to think about his situation. He loved his wife, and he had to find a way to make a break with Vanda now that he realized she was in good hands. But as the days passed, the burden of responsibility for Vanda and his son weighed heavily on him, so he felt the need to call again and again. He even thought of asking a travel agent for information about flights to Brazil. When Dora and the children left again for Greece, Christo encouraged Demetrio to visit his second family. "Take the plane, Demetrio, and go. No one here is going to find out. Just go for a week. You can call Dora from there. She wouldn't know the difference, and when you call her she will think it is from America."

But life was not so clear cut for Demetrio and he was torn with indecision. He called Vanda continually, but could not make the commitment to fly to Brazil. Maybe this way was better, he thought. If he did visit his child and had a chance to bond with him, the separation would be painful. How could he ever leave his child behind?

CHAPTER 7

Summer came, and Demetrio decided to accompany Dora and the children to Greece. He needed a change in his life and felt that a good vacation might relax him. The thought of returning permanently to Greece began once again to gnaw at him. Dora had no reservations about packing everything up and going back to Konitsa, and now that Vanda was gone, Demetrio had no interested in remaining in the United States.

Demetrio hoped that a short trip home would help him forget Vanda. But the opposite happened and she was constantly in his thoughts. Every time Demetrio saw a baby in the streets, his desire to see his own child strengthened. He wondered what his son looked like, and if he resembled his father at all. The harder he tried to forget, the harder it became. He felt helpless and depressed. At times, he dreamt of Vanda, young and beautiful, finding another man, and he was tormented with pangs of misery and jealousy. He cursed himself for not predicting his present situation when he first met Vanda and for allowing things to get out of hand.

As soon as they returned to Culver City at the end of August, Demetrio called Vanda.

"Sweetheart, do you know that on September 17th your son will have his first birthday?" she asked.

"Yes, darling. I know very well because I count each day."

"You should see my parents. They are fighting over who will pick him up. Father no longer goes to the coffee plantation because he wants to spend all the time he can with his grandson."

"Vanda, how about you, my love, how is you life there?" Demetrio wanted to ask if there was another man in her life, but he was terrified that she would say yes, she had found someone else.

"Demetrio, I am fine. Our child is healthy and beautiful and he looks like you. He is also very smart. Imagine, when I talk to him he tries to get out of his crib searching with his eyes to find me. A Greek family lives a block down the street and they have a three-year-old girl called Areti. With them lives also the mother of the wife. My parents know them from a while back. In the summer time, they come over to swim in our pool. I think they come from Athens. When they asked me how we call our baby, I told them Costa. Now both of them call him Costaki. Now we all call him Costaki." Vanda paused for a moment. "Demetrio can you hear me? How come you are not saying anything?" she asked.

"These are such wonderful things you are saying, Vanda. You can't imagine how happy you make me by telling me everything is fine there."

"Now I want to ask you something. Do you promise me that you will be frank with me?"

"Of course I promise. Besides, there is nothing I want to hide from you."

After pausing for a moment, Demetrio asked, "Do you still love me?"

"I would be lying to you if I said that I love you like before. You know Demetrio? I don't like to lie. I want to always tell you the truth? Demetrio's heart raced. Then Vanda said, "I love you even more now. My mind is always with you, day and night. I see the blossom of our love and I want you even more.

I want you holding my hand to be at my side when I take our baby for a walk. I know that this will never happen. I don't want you to leave your family. I knew this from the beginning; this was my fate and my own choice. But I don't complain. Believe me, I have adapted to the situation. If you could only come at least once a year for a few days, it would be the best gift that you could ever give us. I assure you that our Costaki will never have another father besides you."

"Vanda, you cannot imagine the difficulty of my situation."

"Now, Demetrio, let me tell you something else I think you will like very much. Last Sunday we baptized our Costaki in the Greek Orthodox Church of Saint Peter. Thank God we had the help of our Greek neighbors. In the church they were asking us for a birth certificate of the father. Do you know something else, Demetrio? I am preparing, with the priest's help, to also be baptized a Greek Orthodox. Now I will be going to church every Sunday. I am also taking lessons to learn Greek."

"Vanda, are you going to a Greek school?"

"No, Demetrio, a Greek teacher is coming here at the house twice a week to teach me. His name is Giorgos. He is older, but he still is a good teacher. When our son starts talking, I'll talk to him in Greek. What do you think of that?"

"It couldn't have been better. Vanda, now I want to tell you something. A while ago I met another Greek; he is a carpenter. He came to replace some exterior doors in one of my uncle's buildings and we got to talking. His name is also Costa and he came to America about the same time I did. Before that he lived in Brazil for many years. I thought up the idea of having you write me letters in your own language and mail them to his address so he can translate them for me. He is a nice man and very willing to help out. He can also translate my letters to you from Greek to Portuguese. That way I can express myself a little better because my English is horrible, especially the writing. I told Costa our story and he was very moved by it and showed a lot of understanding. He also has an incredible life history of his own. I'll be writing to you shortly and send you his address. What do you think about that?"

"Honey, I think it is great. Now I can send some pictures of your son."

Demetrio felt satisfied now that he had contrived of a better way to communicate with Vanda. In her first letter, Vanda sent him photographs of Costaki and of her parents. He brought the image of his son to his lips and kissed it saying, "My little boy. I have condemned you to be fatherless, my little son."

One afternoon when Demetrio returned from work he found his uncle sitting on the living room couch. He knew that Dora and the children had gone to the movies.

"Good evening, Uncle," he said.

"Oh, hi, Demetrio. How was work today?"

"Everything went well, Uncle. But I am little tired today."

"Sit for a while to rest, Demetrio, and then go take a bath to relax. Have you heard anything from down south? How is your kid?"

"They are fine. The only big problem is that Brazil is too far. Uncle, can we talk about something that affects all of us?"

"Sure we can. What's the problem?"

"As you know, we have always wanted to return to Greece. You know that we have the problem with Dora's father. The old man is living all alone, and at his age it's tough. Do you know what he said to Dora last summer when we were there? 'I am tired of living like a hermit. This is no life; I'd rather be dead.'"

Christo jumped as though a spring coil had come loose

and had pushed him off the couch. “I just can’t believe it, Demetrio. You are driving me nuts. Are you inflicting psychological warfare on me? What you are saying is that Dora’s father can’t live by himself, but you think I can. You are the only real family I have. I thought we had agreed to stay a few more years and then we all go together. I thought we had all agreed on this. Isn’t that right or did I misunderstand you?”

“Uncle, I don’t want you to shout like this. We have to discuss things but we don’t get anywhere when we yell at each other.”

“How can we have a discussion? I don’t think you understand my feelings at all. You know very well that I am tied down here for another couple of years. To sell real estate takes at least that long.”

“Uncle, we understand you and sympathize with you. We don’t want to upset you. We certainly don’t want to pressure you to go back to Greece with us. But you must understand our situation, too. Marianthi is growing up fast. She is now going to junior high. And Anna is right behind her. You know how the school situation is deteriorating daily. We are afraid something bad might happen to the kids. We are afraid of losing them. We want to make the move while we have some control over them. Pretty soon, as they grow up, they will rebel and then they will refuse to come with us. Then we will be condemned to stay here forever in this human jungle. I see what’s happening with our friends’ children and I am terrified.”

Christos was silent. He propped his face in his palms, resting his elbows on his knees and staring at the floor. Finally he said, “Demetrio, you are absolutely right. Look at my own kids. The truth is, around this area things are getting worse. There are so many robberies and other crimes. How can you stop being afraid? I’ll try to sell everything, or else how the hell can we get out of here?”

"Uncle, are you serious? You are going to sell everything?"

Christo grinned and nodded in agreement. "Yeah, I am going to sell the sons-of-a-bitch. Why do I need more wealth if I am going to be all alone?"

Demetrio went to his uncle and put his arms around his shoulder. "Uncle, thank you for your decision. Thank you very much. Dora will be very glad to hear this."

"Demetrio, you know that everything I have will be yours one day. I'll leave something to my own kids, even though they don't care about me at all. I wish I had the guts to cut them off completely, but somehow I can't. I don't want them to curse me after I die."

Demetrio felt better now that his uncle had made a decision, but he also realized that when he returned to Greece, Brazil would be cut off forever. While he loved Dora and the children, he also desired to hold on to his second family. He struggled to find a logical solution, to find a way out of the impasse, but without success. Costaki, his beloved boy, the boy he never had with Dora, pulled him like a giant, invisible magnet.

In the meantime, Christo, true to his promise, signed an agreement with a realtor to dispose of all his real estate holdings. The realtor explained that sales were very slow and that there was no prospect for improvement for another couple of years. Christo explained to Demetrio and Dora that until the market improved, there was nothing he could do. Everything was out of his hands. But Dora made it clear that she would not wait forever. Demetrio tried to console her. "Let's be patient a little longer, Dora. We don't know, something could happen any time."

The next summer, Dora again took the kids and went to be with her father. This gave Demetrio the freedom to talk more often with Vanda. She kept telling him how her parents were crazy about little Costaki. "Your son started taking some steps. Darling, he is almost walking now. My father goes to the farm often and takes him along, too. That gives me some free time and I can go out of the house. You should see how happy he is when he is on the horse and they go for a ride. He loves horses. Father bought him a beautiful white pony. Costaki is crazy about it. Father puts him on the pony and holds him while Costaki holds the reins. Can you believe that? Darling, your son is unbelievable. He wants to stay on the pony and starts screaming when Father tries to get him down."

Hearing these stories about his son made Demetrio want to drop everything and run to Brazil. But he knew he would never go.

When Dora returned from Greece, the first thing she asked was if Christo had had any success in selling his properties. "No Dora. Nothing so far," Demetrio reported.

Every so often Demetrio had to fly back to Vegas. There were always repairs to be done, a door that needed adjustment, or a leaking pipe or broken windowpane that needed to be replaced. All these things he had done with great pleasure when Vanda was there. Now they were nothing but tedious chores. He felt tired of the constant travel, and decided to have a talk with Christo.

"Uncle, I think it would be better to hire a maintenance company to do the work for the Las Vegas building. I think it will be more cost effective to have somebody there instead of me going back and forth, even for little things. What do you think?"

"Yea, I think you are right, Demetrio. Not because it will cost me less, but because it's too tiring for you."

CHAPTER 8

The days, the months, and the years passed by with lightening speed. Christmas was once again upon them. "One more year is almost over," Demetrio thought. "It's been eight full years since I came to America and it seems just like last week."

As the holidays approached, Christo decided to go to Vegas with one of his "girls." Dora had been busy decorating the tree and shopping for presents for days. She tried unsuccessfully to convince Christo to stay and spend the holidays with them. Demetrio was busy with his usual chores, but he did not neglect to find time to buy presents to put under the tree.

"Dora, honey, I'll work only today," he promised as he left in the morning for work. "In two days we have Christmas. Today, I'll come back early so we can go out in the afternoon for any last minute shopping you need."

She kissed him. "Have a good day, honey. We will be here waiting for you. Try to finish up so you don't have to go out tomorrow."

As soon as Demetrio climbed into his truck, his mind flew to his little son and Vanda. "Good thing she has her parents," he said to himself. Then he realized that several days had passed since he had last called. "I must call right away, now that Christmas is coming up. I have to find some convenient time to call," he thought.

That day, Demetrio had to work on his uncle's building in Santa Monica, not far from Culver City. As he worked, he grew increasingly depressed. He felt irresponsible for starting a second family without giving it much thought, but he also felt great jealousy whenever he thought of Vanda finding another man. Slowly, Demetrio began to realize that it was very selfish of him to demand Vanda's devotion. He thought how much easier it would be if he could finally accept that Vanda had a life of her own, far away from him, if he could grant her the freedom to find another man. But at this point, he could not go on. The thought of someone else becoming his son's father was abhorrent to him, was intolerable. "What the hell am I thinking these things for?" he asked himself.

When Demetrio finished the day's chores, he looked at his watch and it was 4:00 in the afternoon. He poured some water on his face from the garden hose to wash off the sweat and then climbed into his truck and headed straight home. As he drove, images of his mother and father appeared in his mind, and he felt unusually close to them. Absorbed in his thoughts, he barely avoided a collision with a trailer truck when he barreled through a red light just a few blocks from his home.

As he approached his driveway, Demetrio noticed several police cars with their lights flashing, a common site in his neighborhood. But as he got closer, he felt his palms grow sweaty and his heart beat faster. Now, he was sure. Something had happened in his own house. His yard was sealed off with yellow police tape, and two officers in dark blue uniforms stood at his door. Several others were walking in his side-yard. "Oh, God, save us from any evil," Demetrio silently prayed.

Just as he reached the foot of his driveway, a policeman stopped him. "I'm sorry sir, you can't go there." Demetrio looked at him puzzled. "This is my home, officer. What's going on? What's all the commotion about?"

The policeman looked at Demetrio carefully. "Do you live in this house?" he asked.

"Yes," Demetrio replied his voice barely audible.

"I am sorry, sir. Leave your car here and come with me."

Demetrio suddenly grabbed the officer's hand. "What's going on? Tell me, is my family okay?"

Without answering, the officer opened the car door and motioned Demetrio to get out. "The officer in charge will explain to you what happened," he said. At that moment, a tall Aframerican policeman in uniform approached Demetrio, took him by the arm and politely asked him to follow. Demetrio followed him as though hypnotized. As they came to one of the police cars that was stopped there, the policeman helped Demetrio into the back seat and he went around to the door on the other side and sat next to him. Demetrio watched the commotion around him and tried to figure out what was going on.

"Sir, I am the officer in charge here and I have to get some information from you," the officer said as he pulled a notebook with a black cover from his pocket. "What is your name, sir?"

"Demetrio Rendis."

"Mr. Rendis, who lives in this house?"

"My uncle, and me with my wife and our two children."

"Where is your uncle, now?"

"He went to Las Vegas to spend Christmas."

"Mr. Rendis, you need a lot of strength for this. I am very sorry that I have to tell you this." Demetrio just stared at the officer.

"Mr. Rendis, a serious crime occurred in your home."

"Crime..." Demetrio's voice echoed. He immediately thought of Dora and the children. "Tell me officer, please tell me, what's going on?"

The police officer put his hand on Demetrio's shoulder. "Mr. Rendis, this is terrible but I have to tell you that somebody killed your wife and your two children."

Demetrio grabbed his head in his hands in desperation. His body and mind went numb, and then he began to cry silently.

"Mr. Rendis, all the evidence indicates that somebody broke in the house to burglarize and it seems that..."

Demetrio could not hear anymore. He opened the car door and walked away. The policeman ran after him. "I am sorry, Mr. Rendis, I wish there is something we can do. We want to help you."

Demetrio continued to move away slowly, his face expressionless, his feet barely lifting off the ground. The policeman caught up to him.

"Mr. Rendis, we have to ask you some more questions," the policeman continued. "I want you to come down to the police station tomorrow morning around 10:00."

"Okay, I'll be there," Demetrio answered.

"And I would like your word that you will not leave town for now." Demetrio nodded in agreement.

Demetrio's ears buzzed. He began to walk quickly to his pick-up truck which was parked a few steps away. He climbed inside, managed to get the key in the ignition, and drove away. As he drove aimlessly, dusk and a light rain began to fall. It made the world seem sad, as sad as Demetrio's soul.

After an hour, Demetrio pulled up to a curb and parked. He leaned his head against the steering wheel, trying to collect his thoughts. But the pain and the immense loneliness that engulfed him got in the way. "Dear God, where are you?" he screamed, raising his hands in desperation. "Do you exist? If you really exist, what are the criteria for your justice?" He continued to rave at his god. " What is the meaning of life?

The end comes the moment somebody decides you should no longer live? Joy and happiness are only a few moments of our life, is that all? Until yesterday I had everything, home, family, children. And then, from one moment to the next, boom... everything has been swept away, forever."

Eventually, Demetrio raised his head and looked around to figure out where he was. At the corner across the street a sign read "Wilshire Boulevard." He couldn't remember having passed through this particular intersection. At that moment, a police car pulled in behind him and turned on its lights. A policeman came around to his side and motioned him to lower the window.

"What are you doing here?" he asked, shining his flashlight directly into Demetrio's eyes. "Don't you see that you are not allowed to park here?" Demetrio did not answer. "Let me see your driver's license and your car registration." After glancing at the documents for a moment, he returned them to Demetrio. "Are you feeling okay, sir?" he asked.

"Yes, officer, I am okay," The policeman hesitated for a moment then said briskly, "Go, and watch where you park your car next time, if you don't want to get a ticket."

"Thank you," Demetrio mumbled as he turned the key in the ignition and took off, again without any particular direction in mind. Some time later, he realized he was driving along Sunset Boulevard. He noticed a crowd standing in front of a night club, one of many in that area. He decided to stop and have a drink. He found the most remote table and ordered. One drink led to another, and after a while the alcohol became his highway to fantasies and dreams. The music blared and short-skirted waitresses passed by every so often dropping off another full glass. Young women came searching for companionship and asked if they could sit next to him. Realizing his disinterest, they quickly left. One woman, holding a drink and smiling, sat down and began caressing his cheek, hoping to arouse his interest. Before long, she too, left. The night wore on, and finally Demetrio pulled out his credit card, paid his bill without checking the amount, and walked out. He was drunk and oblivious to his surroundings. He glanced at his watch but could not make out the time. The hands seemed to be jumping around the watch face like jackrabbits.

As Demetrio walked, the coolness of the night air against his face helped clear his mind and he was able to find his pick-up truck. Again, he drove aimlessly. "What am I going to do now?" he wondered. "My life without my family has no meaning whatsoever." Then in the distance he saw a motel with a VACANCY sign flashing and decided to stop there for the night. The clerk assigned him a room and another helped him climb the few steps to the door and unlocked it for him. Once inside, Demetrio threw himself on the bed without stopping to take off his shoes. He was exhausted and drunk. As he drifted off, he was besieged by nightmares of his murdered family. In his drunken stupor, he couldn't tell if he were still alive or if he had crossed the boundary into the realm of the dead. He saw a swirling cloud and felt himself being pulled out of his body. He saw his mother sat in a corner watching him, silent and sad. From down a dark corridor, he heard his father's voice calling and then saw him beckoming. Demetrio tried to move forward, but a strong force held him back. For several hours, the nightmares continued until he finally woke up terrified and in a sweat. He heard someone knocking at his door. He opened his eyes and couldn't remember where he was. His head felt as if it were about to split open. As he rolled off the bed, he felt very dizzy. With difficulty, he stumbled to the door. "Who is there?" he asked.

"Sir! It's noon. If you want to stay for the day, you have to go down to the lobby and let them know. Otherwise, you must check out now."

"Yeah, I'll go down in a minute," Demetrio answered. He threw some water on his face and suddenly saw a terrified stranger in the mirror looking back at him. His eyes were red and swollen. His unshaven and drawn face made him look like a street bum. "For god's sake, who is that man? Demetrio is that you? No, no, it's not me." He sat on the bed and tried to concentrate. "Where am I?" he asked himself. "Why am I not at home?" Like lightning, the scene at his home flashed through his mind — the police cars with their flashing red and yellow lights, and a crowd of strangers rushing in and out of his home. His mind cleared momentarily and the image of the policeman in charge came to him saying, "A serious crime has occurred."

"My God," Demetrio mumbled desperately. "It's no dream. Dora and my girls are not alive anymore." Demetrio was slowly beginning to face the fact that he was never going to see them again. In his confusion, he tried to figure out who the murderer could be, tried to figure out a way to exact vengeance. Then he calmed down. He recalled Dora's kindness, how she used to collect clothing and deliver it to organizations for the poor. Many times when they were riding in the car together, she would ask him to stop and give a small donation to a homeless person wandering the streets. "I don't think Dora would ask for vengeance," he mumbled to himself. Suddenly, he thought of his uncle, and his grief turned to fury. "He is the cause of this," he thought. "If he had not kept us in this place, we would have gone back to my country and now would be living happily." At that moment, Demetrio hated his uncle. He recalled Christo's big promises, how he told him and Dora that America held great futures for their children. Demetrio started crying. "America buried my children," he thought.

After a while, Demetrio walked down to the motel lobby to straighten out his account. "Sir, how many days do you plan to stay?" asked the clerk at the desk.

"I don't know. You can leave my credit card open and write in the amount when I leave."

Demetrio returned to his room and sat on the edge of the bed. He feebly attempted to plan the next steps in his life but had no idea how to begin. He needed a friend, someone with a clear mind with whom he could share his thoughts and his pain. But after all these years in this city, he had not made even one good, close friend.

Demetrio hadn't taken a bath in two days, so he took his clothes off and stepped into the shower. After dressing again, he went out to his truck and started driving along Sunset Boulevard. He turned onto Hollywood Boulevard looking for some place to eat. His mouth was dry and bitter, his stomach was tied in knots. He parked the truck in an empty lot next to the Grumman's Chinese Theater and walked across the street to a fast-food restaurant. He ordered a burger, French fries and a large soda. He took his tray and went to sit by a window looking out at the traffic on the famous boulevard.

From his window, Demetrio could see people walking by, dressed in all kinds of styles. Young kids, skimpily dressed with no trace of shame, asked for handouts to buy a sandwich. Right outside the door was a large round trashcan. Every once in a while someone would stop and search for something valuable, like a piece of bread or other edible. "This is Hollywood," Demetrio mumbled to himself shaking his head.

Demetrio had heard some unbelievable stories about the magic of Hollywood. Some time ago, he had watched a television program about young people who leave their homes carrying nothing but a suitcase and a bundle of dreams, with just enough money to buy a one-way Greyhound ticket to Hollywood. There, they hope to make it big just like the famous movie stars. Most run out of money quickly, their dreams evaporate, and they find themselves sleeping in alleys and searching through trashcans for food. Some end up as prostitutes or drug dealers.

Suddenly, Demetrio noticed someone standing by his table. He turned and saw a young man with long blond hair, around 17 years old, handsome but filthy.

"Hi, sir. Can you buy me a hamburger? I'm hungry."

Demetrio got up from his seat. "Sure I can. Get two hamburgers, French fries and a large drink, too. Get whatever you like."

The young man looked at Demetrio with surprise. "You are a good man. Thank you, sir. Thank you very much." Demetrio paid and went to sit back at his place. His half-eaten hamburger was still there, as he had very little appetite to finish it. He gathered up the trash from his table, and was about to leave when the young man, his tray full of food, came and sat across from him, smiling proudly as he carried his mountain of food.

"Bon appetite," Demetrio said to him. The young man sat and hungrily started eating. "Do you live here in LA?" Demetrio asked.

"I came from Arizona about three months ago to work in the movies but I had a hard time finding a job. They all say they need experienced people. I found out that the most important thing is to have a good manager. It's hard to talk to anyone without connections. You have to be very lucky to get into the movies. You need to know somebody to get into this business, or to even find somebody to talk to you. If you are lucky, you might run into somebody who is looking for new talent who might give you a chance. I know I have to be patient. I'll wait until the right time comes. In this business you need lots of patience." The young man ate as he talked and the food on his tray was disappearing quickly.

"Do you need some more?" Demetrio asked.

"No, sir. I'm full. Thank you very much."

"Why don't you go back to your home? Don't you have a family in Arizona?"

"Oh, yes. I have my father and my mother. I have a little sister, too. Her name is Melissa. She is waiting for me to settle down here so we can arrange for her to come out also. She wants to become an actress."

Demetrio listened and it dawned on him how easily young people are influenced, and how quickly they can lose sight of reality. He looked at the boy and felt very sorry for him. "Where are you staying now?"

"I stay in a motel with some friends I met here. You want to see where I live?" he said sweetly, and reached out to touch Demetrio's hand.

Demetrio got up abruptly. "I have to go now young man. Good luck to you."

As Demetrio left the restaurant and looked down the street, he noticed Christmas decorations hanging everywhere and he remembered that it was Christmas Eve. He walked across the street to his truck, watching pedestrians walk by.

Demetrio got in his car and drove towards his motel. When he arrived back in his room, exhausted and no longer able to stand up, he fell on his bed and tried to sleep. But whenever he closed his eyes, images of his wife and kids came to torment him. The darkness of the approaching night increased his loneliness and depression. "Tomorrow will be Christmas," he thought, "and I am alone in a motel room. I have no one to turn to for companionship on a day like this."

After tossing and turning for over an hour, he decided to

find a nightclub to help pass the time. He found the credit card receipt from the night before, checked the club's address, and headed out. A few minutes later, he was pulling into the parking lot of the Golden Horse. He resolved that tonight he would permit himself only two drinks.

Inside, the GOLDEN HORSE was in a state of pandemonium. Crowds of young people danced in a delirium induced by the alcohol and music. Many sang along to the songs and everyone held a glass in one hand. Christmas decorations hung from the ceiling. Occasionally, a paper wreath would come floating down and the crowds would stomp on it in glee. The atmosphere resembled that of Mardi Gras. Demetrio could not find a chair at a table so he sat at a barstool. Next to him sat a middle-aged man drinking. He wore a black leather jacket, his tie was loose, and a cigarette hung from his lips throughout the night. Every so often, he would wipe his eyes with the palm of his hand.

Demetrio did not stop at two drinks as he had promised himself. One drink followed another as Demetrio watched the crowds.

When Demetrio finally left the club, he was barely able to walk. It was almost 3:00. Somehow, he made it back to his motel without incident. That night, he slept somewhat better than he had the one before.

CHAPTER 9

Vanda began to worry when Demetrio did not call with his Christmas greetings. The days passed, and still she did not hear from him. Finally, she decided she would have to be the one to call. She asked her father for help. "Daddy, please, you make the call. If a woman answers, say you are a friend of Christo and you want to talk to him," she said. As her father dialed Demetrio's number, Vanda pressed close.

"Hello," a male voice answered. Vanda grabbed the phone from her father's hand. "Demetrio? Demetrio? This is Vanda."

"Vanda, its me, Christo."

"Christo, why don't you say something? Where is Demetrio? Can you hear me?"

"Yes, yes, I can hear you. The problem is I can't really say what happened because I was out of town."

Vanda held her breath so that she could better hear what Christo had to say. She had a premonition that something serious had happened to Demetrio.

"I was in Las Vegas for a few days. I came back yesterday and there was nobody at the house."

"What do you mean, there was nobody home?"

"Vanda, I have a hard time telling you what happened because I can't believe it myself."

Vanda held the phone tightly in her hands and looked at her father with apprehension in her eyes. "What's going on, Vanda?" her father asked. She motioned him to keep quiet.

Finally, Christo spoke again. "Vanda, somebody broke into our house and killed Demetrio's wife and children."

"What?" Vanda fell against her father.

"Sweetheart, what's happening, my little girl?" he asked, taking her in his arms and grabbing the phone. "Christo, this is Vanda's father. Please, tell me what's going on."

"Sir, it's a bad situation here. It appears that robbers broke into the house and, for whatever reason, they shot and killed Demetrio's wife and the two children. This happened a week ago. Since then Demetrio has disappeared. I've been looking everywhere for him. But I have no information."

Vanda sobbed in her father's arms.

"Christo, I have to go, I have to help my daughter. I'll call you again later. If you find out something about Demetrio, please call back again." He helped Vanda to the couch, then grabbed two pillows. Gently, he lifted her head and placed a pillow under it. "Come on, my baby, rest your head so we can see what to do."

Vanda was crying uncontrollably. "Demetrio, poor Demetrio," she said over again. Her father kneeled beside her, held her hand, and gently stroked her hair. When her mother returned with Costaki from the supermarket, she learned the news from her husband and went immediately to console her daughter. Soon, Vanda calmed down and began thinking of what to do next. She told her parents that the best thing would be for her to go to America to find Demetrio.

"I agree, my little girl, and I am willing to do everything possible to find Demetrio," her father answered. "But I think we should wait a while. Maybe Christo can find out something about Demetrio and give us the information we need."

"I think you are right, Dad. Los Angeles is a huge place and it will be difficult to search for Demetrio."

"My little girl, we understand your pain. We are willing to do anything that makes you happy. Our life has no meaning without your happiness."

Vanda took her father's hand and brought it to her face. "Daddy, I love you so much. What would I do without your love and support?" Slowly she got up, took her baby in her arms, and hugged him gently. "My little baby, your daddy is in some kind of trouble," she said crying. "I wonder where your daddy is."

Back in Los Angeles, Demetrio was spending his days wandering aimlessly through the streets, and his nights drinking. After New Year's, he decided to drive over to the police station and make a report as he had been instructed by the police officer. He was not looking forward to this at all because he did not want to see places or people that reminded him of the time he had been happy.

When the officer saw Demetrio enter his office, he got up to greet him. "We were expecting you, Mr. Rendis. Every officer in Culver City is on the lookout for you," he said as he offered him a chair. "You promised me that you would come to the station before now."

"I was sick, sir," answered Demetrio.

"Okay. Okay," the officer said. "Sit down now. I am not going to keep you long. I just have a few questions to ask you."

Demetrio sat, silently.

"Mr. Rendis, first I want to tell you that your uncle stops here almost every day. He is very upset and wants desperately to talk with you to make sure you're all right. He has turned everything upside down to find you. I'll give you his new address. He moved out of the house you used to live in. I think he is trying to sell it."

Demetrio listened without any real interest. He desperately wanted to leave the station, to disappear back into the city. The officer got up, moved closer to Demetrio and said, "We have caught the killers and we will bring them to justice. I hope this brings some relief to you. Personally, I am very pleased to have caught them so fast."

Demetrio turned and asked him, "Why did they kill my wife? What did my children do to deserve this?"

"The killers are members of a local gang. The day they did this, they were under the influence of drugs. Now they are sorry and repent. They want to beg your forgiveness. Your uncle has already seen them and talked to them. Do you want to meet with them, Mr. Rendis?"

"No, sir, it is too difficult for me to face the killers of my family. Besides, why should I see them? I don't think I can ever forgive them. I'll let God forgive them or punish them. He knows what to do."

The officer told Demetrio that his uncle had confirmed the identity of the deceased and had made all the funeral arrangements. Demetrio nodded and tears rolled down his face. "Good-bye, officer," he said, rising to leave. The officer pulled out his business card and handed to him. "My name is Martin Evans. Any time you need something from us, please give me a call. You can always page me."

Demetrio thanked him and walked toward the door.

"Mr. Rendis, where do you live now? We might need to get in touch with you. Also, when your uncle comes by here, what should I tell him?"

"I don't have a permanent residence yet, Mr. Evans – I'm living in a motel. As soon as I rent an apartment, I'll let you know."

When Vanda learned from Christo that Demetrio had reappeared, she calmed down. At least he is alive, she thought.

Now she was trying to find a way to get in touch with him; but how?

"Child, God will help him find a solution," her father told her. "Soon we will hear from Demetrio, I am certain about that." Vanda waited, and hoped.

Demetrio meanwhile lived without any hope or purpose in life. He roamed the streets and shopping malls, returning to the motel when he grew weary. Slowly, he became accustomed to this life and was reluctant to change it. Sometimes he wondered why he was still alive. For years, he had worked hard for his family and his children, so they could have a better life than his own. From the time he had arrived in the USA he had opened up savings accounts for his kids. Now that they were gone, he lived on these savings, and on his credit cards. In the past, he had hated using credit cards because he feared and resented the borrowing trap they tried to lure him into. Now he didn't care. He knew that in America, the bankruptcy law protects debtors and no one is sent to prison for owing money.

One night, as Demetrio was drinking alone in a nightclub, he noticed a young woman leaning against a column near the middle of the room, holding a drink and looking directly at him. He turned quickly away. He was in no mood for female companionship or for any kind of love affair. When the woman saw that Demetrio had noticed her, she walked over to his table. "May I sit here?" she asked pulling out a chair.

Demetrio shrugged his shoulders with indifference.

"My name is Cathy," she said extending her hand.

Demetrio took her hand and allowed himself a slight smile.

"What is your name?" she asked.

"Demetrio."

"That's a cute name. Are you Italian?"

"No, I am Greek."

Cathy asked Demetrio about his life his home country. He responded politely but did not ask any questions back or try to facilitate the conversation. Cathy was about 25, thin, with short blond hair, and beautiful smile. She was also pleasant company. For the first time, Demetrio found himself temporarily distracted from his problems. At one point, Cathy asked if he were married. Demetrio shook his head.

"Do you have a girl friend?"

"None."

Cathy smiled. "A Mediterranean man without a woman is hard for me to believe." She laughed and then she began talking about herself. "I came from Utah about four years ago to find work in computers. I ended up working as a hairdresser instead."

"Why didn't you work in computers? Can't you find a job?"

"Oh, there seem to be plenty of jobs, but for some reason, all the bosses I found were very demanding. They insisted that part of my job was to sleep with them." Cathy gritted her teeth. "And on top of that they weren't that special. Just fat, ugly pigs with rolls of fat under chins as large as their bellies. I hate fat men." She paused for a moment, tightened her lips and looked into her glass. Then she continued. "Demetrio, can we change the subject? Do you want to dance with me?"

"I am sorry, Cathy, but I am depressed and, besides, I am totally ignorant of the new dances. I can only dance tangos, waltzes, or boleros. But nowadays, most people don't even know what those are. It's a shame that the elegance of the past is disappearing."

They kept talking until Demetrio grew weary. Finally he said, "I'm sorry, Cathy, but I am tired, so I'll go. Maybe we'll meet again some other night." He tried to stand up but then sat down again quickly. "Oh, I am dizzy," he said smiling sheepishly.

Cathy took his hand and offered to take him home. “No, I can make it. I don’t think I am that drunk,” he reassured her. Cathy gripped his hand. “I hope we can meet again. Do you know the RAINBOW?”

“Yes, sure. It’s in the sky and appears after the rain.”

“No, not that kind,” Cathy said laughing. “It’s a night club on Sunset Boulevard.” Then she pulled a card out of her purse and wrote the address on the back. “If you ever want to see me, you can meet me there. My card has my home number. You can call me anytime after five in the afternoon.”

Demetrio looked at her seriously. “Cathy, I am in no mood for love affairs, so don’t waste your time with me. I am surprised you don’t have a boyfriend.”

“Yeah, I did and I loved him. Then we broke up.”

“What happened, did you have a fight?”

Cathy did not answer right away. “Demetrio, sometimes I don’t understand people. I knew Mark for almost a year, but as it turned out I didn’t really know him at all. One day I came home earlier than usual because I was not feeling well and I found him in my bed with a man.”

Demetrio shook his head. “Don’t be amazed at anything nowadays, Cathy. The world has changed a lot now. Each person chooses the life that he likes.” Demetrio then got up determined to leave. “Cathy, good-bye,” he said. “I really liked talking to you. I promise, some night I’ll come over to the Rainbow to see you.”

“Remember, I go there after eight. To make sure, call me first.”

“Okay, I will,” he whispered as he went towards the door.

Some days later, Demetrio was lying in bed, staring out his window at the rain that seemed to fall relentlessly. He remembered Dora, the children, his father and mother. He wondered if people really did meet again in heaven. This thought brought him a measure of relief. He thought of his sister and how she, too, was suffering for him and his murdered family.

The rain continued, and Demetrio's thoughts turned to the Rainbow and to Cathy. He had lost count of the days since they had met. He tried to recollect her features, but was unsuccessful. He decided that evening to go visit to Rainbow.

Demetrio arrived there at 10:00. He looked around in hopes of seeing Cathy. It was so crowded and dark that it was hard to recognize anyone standing more than two feet away. He sat at a small table and ordered a drink. After a few hours, when he was about to leave, Cathy came up beside him.

"Demetrio, you are here! How long have been here?"

"I've been here several hours. I was just leaving."

"Every night I've been going to the Golden Horse hoping to meet you there, and then coming here afterwards. Where have you been? I was expecting you'd at least call."

Demetrio searched for an excuse.

"I'll forgive you this first time," Cathy said and put her arm around his. "Come on, now, buy me a beer. Or, don't you like my company?"

"Sure I like your company. I came here today just for you, didn't I?"

That night, it was Demetrio's turn to tell his story. Cathy listened with empathy. At one point, she grabbed his hands and kissed them. "Demetrio, I am so sorry about this. What happened to you is horrible. You must have suffered a lot." Demetrio moved his chair next to hers and put his arm around her. "When this happened, Cathy, I lost control. I was so depressed that I came close to losing my own life. I considered suicide but I was afraid to do it. Despite what people say, you need a lot of strength to do it and I felt powerless. Then I started drinking, something I've never done before in my life."

When Demetrio talked about living in a motel room, Cathy shook her head. "No, Demetrio, I will not let you stay in a motel, alone. I have a small apartment in Westward. You come and stay as long as you want. What do you say?"

Demetrio stroked her hair. "You are a nice girl, Cathy. I have a feeling we will get along." Then he kissed her on the cheek.

Cathy pulled Demetrio closer and kissed him on the lips. "I like you, Demetrio. I liked you from the very first moment I met you. "

Later when they walked out of the club, Cathy asked him to follow her in his truck. In less than 15 minutes they had arrived at her place. She showed him where to park and, arm-in-arm, they walked up the few steps to her door. It was then that Demetrio noticed Cathy's beautiful green eyes. Cathy stepped inside, put her arms around Demetrio's waist and kissed him. "Welcome to your new home, Demetrio," she said. Then, holding him by the arm, she showed him around. In the small living room was a couch. "Sit Demetrio. I'll make some coffee."

Demetrio immediately felt better being away from the lonely and depressing motel room. He had missed human companionship. When Cathy brought the coffee, Demetrio was already half asleep. She sat next to him. "You are very sleepy, Demetrio. Would you like to sleep with me?" she asked. Demetrio nodded. Cathy snuggled close to him and stroked his hands. When she finished her coffee, she got up and went into her room. She returned with only a large towel wrapped around her. Demetrio was attracted to her nice figure and shapely legs. She went close to him, sat on his knees, kissed him: lightly, and reassured him; "I am not going to take long, Demetrio."

The short time that Cathy was in the shower was sufficient

for Demetrio to lie back and fall asleep. Cathy came out singing softly and saw him sleeping. She took his shoes off, covered him with a blanket, and went to bed.

It was noon before Demetrio woke up. He opened his eyes, and glanced quickly around the room. He remembered that he was no longer at the motel. He got up and went to Cathy's room, but it was empty. On her bed he found a note saying: "Demetrio, I went to work and will be back at 4:00. Get something to eat from the refrigerator. Tonight we'll eat out at a Greek restaurant in the Valley. I am sure you'll like it. P.S., Tonight you'll be my guest. Call if you need anything. The door key is hanging on the inside of the door. You can keep it – I have another one for myself. See you later, Cathy."

Suddenly, Demetrio felt the world around him changing. He returned to the motel to check out and then headed back to Cathy's apartment. On the way, he passed the Westside Pavilion shopping mall and decided to stop and buy some clothes. When Cathy returned home that day, she found Demetrio clean-shaven and dressed. "Demetrio! You are very handsome," she exclaimed. She put her arms around his neck and kissed him. Demetrio hugged her tightly and then together they sat on the couch. Demetrio saw her bright eyes sparkle with excitement and realized how pleased she was that he was there.

"Tell me what you did today," she asked.

Demetrio smiled. "Nothing in particular. I checked out of the motel and bought some new clothes from a nice men's store. Then I came here to wait for you."

Cathy kissed him again, this time more intensely. "Demetrio, I want you," she said passionately. "Take me to bed."

Later that evening, they drove over to the Valley. "How do you know this Greek restaurant?" asked Demetrio.

"At the hair salon where I work I got to know a Greek

woman named Sofia. She told me about it. Demetrio, tell me something about Greece. I've heard so many good things about it, about its beautiful islands."

"Cathy, I am from the north part of the country, I have not been to any of the islands."

"Demetrio, can we go for a vacation to Greece?"

Demetrio didn't reply.

"What do you say, Demetrio, can we go?"

"Cathy, at this time I have so many problems, I haven't had time to think about a vacation or any other pleasure for that matter."

"At least tell me something about your country. About the part of the country you come from. And promise me that one day we'll go there together."

"Cathy, I don't make promises unless I am sure I can keep them."

"Then I'll take you to see Utah. It's beautiful there. You'll also get to meet my family. You know Demetrio, close to my home there is a beautiful lake that is very famous because its water is salty. There are beautiful places in Utah. A lot of tourists visit there in the spring and the summer."

Demetrio smiled. "Near my home in Konitsa —that's the name of my home town where I was born and grew up– there is a beautiful river with crystal clear water. This river is called Aoos. That's where my friends and I learned how to swim when we were young. Nature has been very generous to my hometown. The weather is mostly mild, and even the winters there are beautiful. There are a lot of natural springs and the land is very green and brilliant, especially in the spring when the wildflowers are in bloom. The people are also very hospitable and pleasant. Yet, tourism, for better or for worse, has not yet developed as much as it could." Then he smiled.

"Why are you smiling?" she asked him.

"Because I remember when we were swimming in the river with my friends, all naked. It was a great and exhilarating feeling, a feeling of freedom, just like the birds. I have the most pleasant memories from my childhood years, growing up. That's where I met the young girl I later married." His face darkened. "If she only knew what was going to happen to her."

Realizing the depth of Demetrio's grief, Cathy continued to drive in silence. The only sound came from the soft hum of the car's engine.

That night was unforgettable for Demetrio. He realized that Cathy was very happy and easily pleased. She heartily drank Greek resinated wine and delighted in listening to the Bouzouki, a traditional Greek instrument. "Demetrio, please teach me how to dance," she said pulling him to the floor. "I want to learn Greek dancing." Demetrio smiled at her enthusiasm and, with his arms around her shoulder, tried to teach her the rhythm and basic steps of the Calamatiano and Sirto dances.

When they left the restaurant that evening, Cathy placed her car keys in Demetrio's palm. "Demetrio, you drive. I am a little dizzy tonight." On the way home, Cathy leaned her head against Demetrio's shoulder and gradually drifted off to sleep.

As the days passed, Demetrio's depression began to wane. Cathy's understanding and gentleness worked like magic to restore good feelings in his heart and to ease the pain and suffering of the previous months. "I'll try to find a job," he told himself one day with conviction. "Whatever kind of job." He felt uncomfortable that Cathy was working while he spent his days idling around. But Cathy understood his trauma and encouraged him to take time to heal, to rebuild his confidence and his strength. Every day after Cathy returned from work, they would walk together to Clover Park, a large shaded park with exercise equipment and running trails. Cathy was in very good shape, and could easily run five miles a day. Demetrio quickly adjusted to her lifestyle and respected her advice and decisions. Before meeting her, he had never exercised regularly. Now, he found himself enjoying their daily runs, and felt that they were good, not only for his body, but also for his mind and spirit.

"Don't rush into any job with which you are not completely satisfied," Cathy told him. "It's important that first you feel good before you get a job. We have money for rent and food." Then, spontaneously, she put her arms around his neck. "Oh, Demetrio, my baby Demetrio. I met you and you brought joy to my life. Life now is full of meaning. I love you. I love you so very much."

Demetrio's outlook on life changed dramatically. He felt it was worthwhile to be alive. He went out and, after several interviews, found a job in a flower shop nearby. This job was very different from the dirty, heavy labor he had been doing for his uncle. His new job was easy and clean. He spent his time in the shop helping customers choose flower arrangements, or cleaning and preparing flowers as they came in from the farms. His pay was not that great, but it covered his personal expenses. And every day he brought home flowers for Cathy; – sometimes a red rose, sometimes a pretty pink carnation, sometimes a gardenia, fragrant and white.

CHAPTER 10

As time went on, Demetrio pulled out from the dark loneliness and doubt that had engulfed him and began to feel content. Often, he thought of the Chinese saying that one must address all serious problems with immediacy and vigor, like a person who has fallen through a frozen lake. Demetrio became determined to escape from the frozen lake into which his misfortunes had thrown him.

Cathy was also very pleased to see Demetrio improve with time. Happily, their personalities complemented each other and their friendship and understanding grew stronger as they spent more time in each other's company. Cathy was a good cook so they often ate at home. She loved to set the table with colorful cloths, two lighted candles, and a good bottle of wine. Sometimes, after dinner, she would sit on Demetrio's lap, playing her guitar, and singing songs from her hometown. Stroking his hair gently, she would say to him, "America is not the jungle you see in Los Angeles. When we go to Utah one day, you will see a completely different world from the one you know. There is hardly any crime there. People are very friendly and there is a lot of neighborhood dancing clubs where people go on Saturday nights. Also, I want to take you to Kentucky to meet my uncle, my father's brother, who lives there. He has a big farm near Lexington where he breeds thoroughbred horses."

Demetrio raised his eyebrows in wonder and exclaimed, "What kind of work is this? I have no idea what this is."

Cathy tried to explain her uncle's profession as best as she could. "He mates thoroughbred horses and then sells the foals to people who train them for racing. There are many other breeders in that area of the state."

"Your uncle must be well off?"

"His family lives comfortably. Although, from what I hear, many farmers go bankrupt. It's a risky business. What I remember most about my visits is riding the different horses. I loved being with those horses."

"Demetrio, I'll tell you something you won't believe. When I was a child, I could talk with horses; not with all of them, but with some. Horses are very smart. Many people believe horses have human intelligence."

"Tell me, how can you talk with a horse?"

"I stand in front of him. I put my arm around his neck and I ask questions. When the horse agrees with me, he moves his head up and down. When he disagrees, he shakes his head sideways."

Demetrio laughed. "Maybe it's true. I can't say because I never had any contact with thoroughbreds. When I meet them, I'll try and do as you say. Maybe I can teach them Greek."

Cathy laughed. "Imagine, my uncle's horses will be bilingual."

In the second week of May, Cathy and Demetrio took two weeks vacation from their jobs to travel to Utah and then to Lexington to visit her uncle. They flew into Salt Lake City. To surprise her parents, Cathy did not call them ahead of time. When she and Demetrio got there, no one was home. After talking to the neighbors, she found out that her parents had gone to Florida and were not coming back till the end of May.

"That's a shame," she told Demetrio. "I wanted you so badly to meet them." They decided to stay in Salt Lake for one day, just enough time for Demetrio to see some of the city with its clean streets, expansive green spaces, and the salty lake nearby.

The friendliness of the people and the beauty of the land, especially the birds, impressed Demetrio. "I never imagined, Cathy, that such colorful birds existed right here," Demetrio said that night as they were eating dinner on the patio of a restaurant. "I always thought they were confined in zoos or in exotic lands far from civilization."

Large trees circled the patio and their leaves rustled softly in the cool breeze. The night was dark, and stars sparkled against the deep black sky.

"When I was in school, Demetrio, I loved to read about birds," Cathy said. "I learned about homing pigeons trained to deliver messages. I was amazed that they could fly such great distances. They won't interrupt their flight for anything – they'll even fly through thunderstorms or even hurricanes. The only thing that can stop them is a preying hawk – a pigeon's natural enemy. Brazil is a great place for birds," she continued. "It's famous for its colorful parakeets and the amazing black 'maina' whose song sounds very much like a human voice."

At the mention of Brazil, thoughts of Vanda and Costaki suddenly flooded violently through Demetrio's mind. "God," he thought to himself, "why haven't I thought of them all this time?" He began counting the years since he last saw Vanda and was amazed when he realized that Costaki was about three years old.

Cathy immediately sensed that something had disturbed Demetrio. "What is it, Demetrio? Did I say something wrong?"

He looked at her with sadness. "Cathy, there's something I think I must tell you. I had no intention of keeping it from you, and I should have told you earlier, but with all my past troubles it just went by."

Cathy took Demetrio's hands and said calmly, "Whatever is bothering you, you can always tell me."

"When I was visiting Las Vegas several years ago, I met a very special girl from Brazil. Her name is Vanda. That's why, when you mentioned Brazil, I thought of her."

Cathy tightened her grip on his hands. "Tell me, Demetrio, I want to know, what happened next?"

After a moment, Demetrio continued. "I have a child with her. When she left for Brazil, she was two months pregnant. I know my child only through photographs. I want you to know that from the first time I met her she knew I was married. I never gave her any hope of us having a future together. She wanted to have a child with me before going back to her country. Her family is well off, so I have never been concerned regarding financial support."

Cathy, who had been listening intently, suddenly seemed pleased. Demetrio was surprised. "Cathy, you are not mad at me?" he asked.

She shook her head. "No Demetrio. It's a beautiful story. Tell me, do you love her?"

"I think I love her. You see, it's also the child that's binding us together."

"Do you keep in touch? Have you told her about what happened to you?"

"No, not yet. When the tragedy happened, I was out of my mind and I couldn't get my thoughts together. There were times when I was not sure if I was alive or if I was trapped in a nightmare. Believe it or not, even now it is hard for me to convince myself that my family is gone forever." Demetrio buried his face in his hands to hide the tears that swelled in his eyes.

Cathy looked at him compassionately. "Demetrio, I am with you and I want to do anything I can to lessen your pain."

"Thank you, Cathy. I really don't know what I would have done without you. You came into my life when I really needed you. God must have sent you."

After one day in Utah, they took another flight to Lexington, Kentucky. The four-hour flight time went by fast. During the flight, Cathy tried to convince him that he should take some actions to straighten out his life. "If Vanda is not involved with someone else, you should seriously consider getting together with her and your child."

"Cathy, I want to thank you for your kind words. I will never forget what you have done for me."

Cathy was a woman who wanted to live life fully, experiencing everything life had to offer. She enjoyed friendships and love affairs with men, without desiring the attachment of marriage or children. She believed there would be plenty of time for all that later. She only felt physically attracted to Demetrio. When she had first learned about his tragedy, she had wanted to help get him back on his feet. Now that she knew about Vanda, she felt confident that she could help him patch up his life, and that everything would work out fine in the end.

"Demetrio, we'll be there in about an hour," Cathy said. "When we fly over Lexington you will see how beautiful the city looks from the air. Once I flew here at night with my father and it looked fantastic. It felt like the earth was studded with millions of little lights."

Suddenly, the stewardess came over the intercom, announcing their descent into Lexington.

"Demetrio, we have arrived," Cathy said holding his hand tightly.

"Your hands are cold," Demetrio observed.

Cathy smiled awkwardly. "Yeah, it always happens to me when I fly. Especially during landing or take off. It's probably my nerves. It never happened to me when I was young," she said.

A few minutes later, the turbines moaned, and the wheels hit the ground. The huge mass swayed from side to side and rumbled like a tree-leaf resisting the maddening fury of the winter wind.

Cathy slowly raised her head and looked at Demetrio smiling.

CHAPTER 11

As soon as they were out of the airport building, they took a taxi and within a half-hour were at Cathy's uncle's farm. Demetrio could not stop looking around in wonder. The property, made up mostly of green pastures was vast, enclosed by miles of white wooden fencing that gleamed in the sunlight. A winding path led from the road up to the highest knoll, where a beautiful, two-story farmhouse stood. A dozen horses grazed in the distance, oblivious to the visitors' arrival.

"How do you like it?" Cathy asked.

"It's so beautiful. Only in paintings have I seen something like this." Demetrio took the larger of the two suitcases and left the small one for Cathy to carry. They turned toward the house and saw a man walking towards them down the path. As he approached, his pace quickened.

"Cathy!..." he cried coming up to them. "Welcome, welcome." and giving his niece a great big hug. He was a man of about 50, reddish-blond, tall, and strong, with a bushy red mustache. He wore brown boots, a checkered shirt and a cowboy hat tied with a string around his chin.

"Uncle, this is my friend Demetrio."

"Demetrio, welcome to our home. My name is Steve Morrison," Cathy's uncle said as he took a good look at Demetrio and extended his hand for a hearty shake.

"Nice to meet you, Mr. Morrison."

"Where are you from Demetrio?"

"I am from Greece."

"Greece? That's a very pleasant surprise, Demetrio. The birthplace of civilization and democracy, Aristotle, Pericles, Hippocrates. That's what I remember about Greece from my school days." He took the suitcase from Cathy and put his arm around her shoulder. "Let's go in now to greet your aunt. She will be very happy. It's been years since the last time you were here." Before he had the chance to say another word, Cathy left them and ran up the path in excitement.

"Demetrio, how did you decide to visit us?"

"It was Cathy's idea. We first went to her home in Utah but unfortunately there was nobody home because her parents were vacationing in Florida."

"What kind of work you do, Demetrio?"

Demetrio hesitated for a moment, then said, "I do all kinds of work. Now I work in a flower shop."

When they arrived at the house, Cathy and her aunt were waiting for them at the doorstep. "Come Demetrio, I want you to meet my Aunt Susanna."

"I am very pleased to meet you, Aunt Susanna," Demetrio said.

"Welcome to our home, Demetrio!" Then she turned to Cathy. "I like it when he calls me 'Aunt Susanna.'"

Susanna was tall, with blue eyes, blond hair that had begun to turn gray, and rosy cheeks. She wore short boots, and a long colorful dress and leather belt decorated with a shiny brass buckle much like her husband's.

After they exchanged a few pleasantries, Cathy took Demetrio by the arm and led him out the back door to the stables.

Suddenly she stopped and asked, "Do you know how to ride a horse?"

"How should I know?" Demetrio replied laughing. "Where I grew up we only had donkeys to ride. My family's donkey was called Kitso. Many times when I was young, I'd ride him out to our little farm yard near our home to cut fresh vegetables for my mother to cook." Demetrio paused. "What a beautiful time that was when I was a child. How did the years go by so fast?"

Cathy approached the first in a series of stables that lined the far side of the farm. She opened the short gate and entered. A moment later she returned, holding a reddish-brown horse by the reins. Demetrio leaned on the nearby wooden fence and watched her. With a quick step and a jump Cathy was suddenly on the horse. "You are not going to use a saddle?" Demetrio asked.

Cathy laughed. "I prefer to ride bareback," she explained. " I feel much more freedom that way." Then she pulled at the reins and leaned her body forward. The horse lifted up his front legs, neighed, and galloped away, faithfully obeying Cathy's commands.

After taking a few passes around the open pasture, Cathy returned to the gate where Demetrio was still standing. With one quick jump she was on the ground again. Her cheeks were flushed and her eyes sparkled. "How did I look?" she asked giving Demetrio a quick kiss.

Demetrio smiled broadly and hugged her. "I cannot believe it, Cathy. You are a wonderful rider.

Still holding the horse by the reins, Cathy leaned her head against Demetrio's chest and asked, "How many days do you think we should stay here?"

"We can stay as long as you want."

Cathy lifted her eyes and smiled slyly. "We have one little problem here," she said.

"What do you mean?"

"Well, as long as we are here, we can't sleep together. My aunt and uncle are pretty conservative when it comes to that."

"Well, I think it's proper to respect our host's rules," Demetrio replied smiling.

The next morning when Demetrio woke up, he looked out the window and saw an amazing sight. The rolling hills were green with grass and studded with towering trees, and the sky was crystal clear and blue, just like in Konitsa. But what most impressed Demetrio was the lush, shimmering blue-green of the famous Kentucky bluegrass that grew in the fields.

In the evenings, Cathy and Demetrio would take her uncle's car and drive downtown to the nightclubs, which were very different from the ones Demetrio had come to know and despise in Los Angeles. People were much more friendly and courteous. They danced together without groping each other provocatively or kissing passionately on the dance floor. Men wore blue jeans, boots, and cowboy hats. Women wore jeans or long, colorful dresses. The music was new, too, for Demetrio – melodic, without the driving rhythms that irritated his eardrums. "That's country music, Demetrio," Cathy explained as she took him to a corner and tried to teach him the two-step.

Time passed quickly for Demetrio, too quickly. He had little desire to return to Los Angeles. No one was waiting for him there, and he was enjoying his time on the farm. Each morning, Cathy and Demetrio would go out riding. The first time Demetrio got on a horse he worried that he wouldn't be able to stay on the saddle. Gradually, he got used to it, and even worked up to a gallop. But in the evening, after every ride, his body hurt from the exertion. Cathy watched him closely and gave him tips, and laughed good-naturedly at his inexperience. It didn't take long before Demetrio could keep up and ride along beside her. Sometimes they would race, making bets as to who could be first to reach the stables.

"You made a lot of progress, and I see you are beginning to like horses," Cathy said one day.

"To be honest with you, Cathy, I never imagined that horseback riding could be such fun. Do you know how I feel? Like I am breaking an invisible barrier and am passing through into a new world; a good world, without the usual responsibilities and hang-ups. I feel carefree. The only thing I have not accomplished yet is to be able to have a conversation with one of the horses."

Cathy smiled and kissed him, stroking his rich dark hair. "Demetrio, in the few days we have left, I'll take you around to Lexington to see the sights. We might also stop in a motel."

Demetrio hugged her tightly. "I agree. That would be really nice. You always have great ideas."

"Now, Demetrio, I will give you a short history lesson on this beautiful place called Kentucky. It was the 15th state to join the Union on June 1, 1792. Kentucky is a Cherokee Indian word. It probably means 'Land of Tomorrow' or 'Meadowland.' The origin of the Cherokee tribe, Demetrio is a mystery even to Cherokees themselves. I am sure that they did not drop down from the clouds or spring up from the earth as some of their ancestors believed. Indians lived in this area for 15,000 years. Kentucky is also called 'The Dark and Bloody Ground.'"

"Why?" asked Demetrio.

"Because of the fierce battles and amount of blood that was shed here during the Civil War. The two men who were president at the time, Abraham Lincoln of the North and Jefferson Davis of the South, were both born in Kentucky, less than 100 miles apart. Isn't that weird?"

"Cathy, all the things I learn are very interesting. Tell me, how many people live in Kentucky now?"

"A little less than four million. Kentucky has some wonderful sights. There's a place called Cumberland Falls, near Corbin. The Cumberland River is about 125 feet wide there, and drops into a 65-ft waterfall. It's fantastic. Thousands of people come to visit the waterfall every year. There's also Mammoth Cave, about 110 miles south of Lexington. It's a huge system of underground caves. And then there's the land between the lakes – a large park sandwiched between two lakes near the Tennessee border. It has more than 170, 000 acres. I wish we could visit it but it's a little too far."

"How far is it?" asked Demetrio.

"It's about 200 miles from here."

"Then let's plan for it some other time."

"Will there be another time?" Cathy asked, not looking at him.

Demetrio did not reply.

After a few moments, Cathy spoke again. "Kentucky has quite a few universities and colleges. The largest is Kentucky University here in Lexington. It has about 24,000 students. Kentucky produces more whiskey than other states in America and is the biggest producer of tobacco in the world. And Lexington, of course, is the breeding place of some of the best racing horses in the world. Our racetrack, Churchill Downs, is near Louisville, the biggest city in the state. Each May, it hosts the famous Kentucky Derby. The Derby started back in 1875. More than 10,000 people came to see a horse named Aristides take the first title. Nowadays, about 130,000 people come to the track on race day, and millions watch the Derby on TV. By the way, all the horses at the Derby are three years old."

Demetrio interrupted her. "Cathy, can I ask you something?"

"Sure, you can ask me anything."

"How can you remember all these things in such great detail, with dates, and everything?"

"When I was in school I loved history. I have so many books in my house that it looks like a public library. But, I also have good memory, so whatever I read, I remember it forever. One of my history teachers told me once that I have a photographic mind."

Demetrio kissed her. "You not only have a photographic mind, but you are also a wonderful person. If I didn't have the good fortune to run across you, I don't know where I would be now. I want to thank you for all you have done for me." Cathy said and leaned into Demetrio's arms.

CHAPTER 12

When Cathy first met Demetrio, she thought she was entering into nothing more than a short-term adventure. But as time passed, she came to feel close to this man who seemed serious, courteous, giving, and honorable. Now, she felt that she might be falling in love with him. She tried to explain her feelings away as nothing more than the excitement of having a relationship with a man whom she knew she ultimately couldn't have, a man who belonged to another woman. Cathy knew that Demetrio loved Vanda and his son, and she believed that one day he would return to them. She also thought it would be wrong of her to try to keep him from them, even though she now desired this very much.

The following morning after breakfast, Cathy and Demetrio went for their daily ride. Later, as they were driving into town, Demetrio noticed that Cathy was deep in thought.

"What's the problem, Cathy?" he asked.

"Oh, nothing. I think I had a tough time falling asleep last night. That's all."

Demetrio dropped the subject but watched her closely for a hint of what might be troubling her. To break the silence, he asked, "What's on the agenda for today?"

"Last night, after you went to bed, I looked through one of the many Kentucky guidebooks my uncle keeps in his book shelf. I think we should go see the house of Mary Todd, Abraham Lincoln's wife. On the way back, we can stop by the cemetery, which is nearby. Although I don't usually like cemeteries, I think this one is interesting because it's filled with beautiful gardens and wildflowers. That's where the Todds, Mary Lincoln's parents, are buried. There are also many other famous Americans buried here. One of them is the Southern Civil War general John Hunt Morgan who helped win many battles against the Yankees. He was killed in 1864 in a battle near Greenville, Tennessee, along with many of his soldiers, when they were surrounded by the opposing troops. General Morgan had also distinguished himself as a young volunteer soldier in the Mexican-American War. The cemetery is filled with veterans from the South and the North."

As Cathy drove, Demetrio touched her hand. "You are the most beautiful teacher I ever met," he said and leaned to touch her head with his.

Cathy felt confused, but she smiled. "Thank you Demetrio. It's nice that at least you find me beautiful."

"Now, my good teacher, tell me something about the famous Abraham Lincoln's life."

Cathy pursed her lips for a moment. "There are so many things one can say about Lincoln. If America is a great, unified nation today, it is because Lincoln believed it was important to keep the nation intact. He was born on February 12, 1809 at a place called Sinking Spring Farm near Hodgenville about 100 miles southwest of Lexington. His father's name was Thomas Lincoln and his mother's Nancy Hanks. Lincoln lived there till he was seven years old. Then, his father moved the family to Southern Indiana. A couple of years later, his mother died and his father married Sarah Johnson. Abraham Lincoln learned many good things from his father. He learned to be honest, to work hard, love learning, and most of all to have unwavering faith in God. Later he studied law and at a young age he entered politics. Practically penniless, he went by himself to New Salem, a small town in Illinois. He was essentially self taught. Working as a clerk, he was able to make a living and support himself. He became very adept at using the English language and became a skillful political orator. In 1837, Lincoln went to Springfield, Illinois. There, a few years later, he married Mary Todd. Together they had four children but only one, Robert, who was the oldest, survived to adulthood. The other three died when they were still young. Lincoln remained in Springfield until 1861 when he was elected the 16th president of the United States."

Demetrio listened to Cathy quietly and intently. He was very impressed by her knowledge and ability to tell a good story. Finally, Cathy paused and turned to look at him. "Demetrio, do you enjoy hearing Lincoln's story?"

"Oh, yes. I love to learn these things. I had the impression that America was a relatively new country and had very little interesting history."

"Well, our written history certainly isn't as old as yours – Europeans settled here only about 500 years ago."

"Cathy, I promise to go out and buy books to learn more about American history."

"You don't need to buy books. If you go to a public library, you will find all kinds of books. I'll help you." Then Cathy stopped the car by the side of the road and pointed to a house across the street. "This is the house that belonged to the Todd family. Mary Todd was born here. Her nickname was Molly." They continued along West Main Street, until they reached the Lexington Cemetery. For the first time in his life, Demetrio saw a cemetery that resembled a large beautiful garden. It was brimming with trees and flowers, very different from the sad, dreary graveyards that lay in the shadow of melancholy cypress trees that he had known in his youth in Greece. As they walked back to the car, Demetrio wrapped his arms around Cathy. "Cathy, I am hungry," he said. "Can we sit some place and eat?"

Cathy nodded. A few minutes later, they stopped at an Italian restaurant and ordered some food and wine. Cathy tried to appear happy, but Demetrio sensed her unease. "Is there anything else you want to tell me about Lincoln's life?" he asked.

"What else can I say, Demetrio? He died when he was only 56 years old. His life ended because some cruel people decided that he should no longer live. He was assassinated on April 14, 1865, while watching a play at Ford's Theater in Washington. History says that his killer was a disturbed actor by the name of John Wilkes Booth. But more than 130 years after his death, we still don't have all the answers. Some strange things happened at the time of his death – the telegraph office in Washington stopped working, and his bodyguard who was supposed to be by his side had disappeared. The bodyguard was never called to testify in court. And right after the murder, the police blocked every road leading out of Washington, which was a small city at the time. But Booth still managed to escape with help from his supporters. When his diary, who was kept secret for years, finally made public, several pages were missing. In 1974, an appraiser was going through the personal papers of Lincoln's Secretary of War, and found the missing pages. They listed the names of seventy high-ranking government officials, army officers, police, and wealthy merchants. In 1865, during the investigations into Lincoln's assassination, more than 2,000 people were interrogated. Finally, the authorities concluded that seven men and one woman conspired with Booth to kill the president. Four of those men were convicted to life in prison; the other three men and the woman were hanged. Some people believe that the witnesses who testified against the accused were bribed with huge amounts of money. A few days after Lincoln was killed, army troops in Virginia caught and killed a man named James William Boyd who greatly resembled Booth and who had tattooed on his arm the initials JWB, just like Booth had. Everyone believed then that the body of Boyd was Booth's. As an American, Demetrio, I would not hesitate to give my life for my country. But many times I am very disappointed with what I see happening around me. When I was in school and learned the story of Lincoln's assassination, I was shocked. And I know many other American schoolchildren feel the same. Even though more than 130 years have passed since the time of Lincoln's death and none of the 30 million Americans who lived at that time is still alive, Lincoln's soul is still with us. Whenever I pick up a book about Lincoln, I feel as if he's standing there, next to me. What is sad about it is that these things still happen in our own time. In 1963, another American president, John F. Kennedy, was killed. He was only 46. He was probably the best-loved president after Lincoln. Just like Lincoln's assassination, Kennedy's assassination has left many doubts and unanswered questions. To this day, the American people do not know with certainty who killed Kennedy. One day, maybe our great-grandchildren will learn the whole truth."

Cathy paused. Her hands were clasped together, and she twirled her fingers nervously. Suddenly, she looked at Demetrio.

"What do you say Demetrio? Shouldn't we get going?"

Without saying a word, he got up and took her hand. "Let's go, honey. I just want to see you happy. Come on; put on a happy face for me. That's it!" He bent over and kissed her.

"I don't want to see you sad. Besides, all these things happened a long time ago. And don't forget, that's how history is made," said Demetrio, as they came out of the restaurant, holding hands.

They walked around to the back of the restaurant where the car was parked. Before getting in the car, Cathy stopped and kissed him. A little later, on the way home, Cathy pulled up in front of a motel. Demetrio looked at her, pleased. He wanted to tell her how much he wanted to sleep with her, but he feared that she would think that sex was all he wanted.

Cathy looked at him and smiled, squeezing his hand tightly.

CHAPTER 13

After spending a week in Lexington, Demetrio and Cathy decided to rent a car and take a quick tour of Kentucky. On the first day, they stopped at Hodgenville to visit the Abraham Lincoln Birthplace National Historic Site. Then, they drove 100 more miles to Bardstown where they stopped for a drink. Throughout the trip, Cathy told Demetrio wonderful stories about Kentucky's past, and Demetrio was convinced that not even a professional tour guide could have done a better job. As they were sipping their drinks outside of a convenience store at a rest stop along the Blue-Grass Parkway, Cathy cried out.

"What happened, Cathy? Is anything wrong?" Demetrio asked.

"Do you see that train on the billboard across the street? The one that says 'My Old Kentucky Diner Train?'"

"Sure I see it."

"Do you know what it is, Demetrio?"

"Of course not!"

"Neither do I, really, since I've never been here before in my life. But a friend of mine came here for her honeymoon and said she was enchanted with this train."

Demetrio crossed his arms and said with a smile, "Please tell me what impressed your friend the most."

"She told me that it's a 1940s dinner-train with a three-wagon restaurant. Each day, it takes passengers on a two-hour dinner tour through the countryside. All the food is cooked in the train's kitchen and is supposed to be delicious."

"It sounds very interesting", Demetrio said.

"Since we are here, Demetrio, we should take the tour."

"I agree with you, *koukla*."

"*Koukla*, what does that mean?"

"*Koukla*, darling, means doll."

"From now on, Demetrio, call me *koukla*."

"Whatever you like, *koukla*."

Cathy smiled. "I wish our vacation would never end."

"Me too. I really love your company."

"Now, Demetrio, wait here a minute while I go buy a tour guide of this area."

Demetrio watched her disappear into the gift shop. He shook his head and smiled. "She is a real *koukla*," he thought.

In a few moments Cathy came running back. "Demetrio, let's go. I found what I wanted," she said waving her guidebook. "You can drive and I'll navigate. The train station is pretty close by. We can take the next tour out. Is that all right?"

"Well, it would be more romantic at night," Demetrio replied.

"Maybe I will never get married," Cathy suddenly said quietly. "But at this moment, I feel so happy being with you, and I've had such a beautiful time the last few days that I feel like I'm on a honeymoon and it's the best one I could ever hope to have." She turned to look at him. "Thank you, Demetrio. I want to thank you so much for the beautiful time we have spent together."

"You promised me you'd never cry again."

"But I am not crying," Cathy said, trying unsuccessfully to hold back her tears.

When they reached the station, there were already many people waiting. Cathy told Demetrio to find a parking spot and she quickly got out of the car. She went to the end of a long line and asked an elderly woman. "It this where we wait to buy tickets?"

"No, young lady. I bought these tickets two days ago. We are waiting here to get on board."

Cathy ran like a bullet towards the ticket window where another long line had formed. When her turn came, she asked for tickets. "For what day?" responded the ticket seller, a blond young man about 30 years old with strange green eyes.

"For today, if possible."

He smiled. "This must be your first time to Bardstown."

"Yes, this is my first time."

"Tickets sell out quickly for these tours and you have to buy them a few days in advance," the seller explained. "Are you by yourself?"

"No, I am with my husband. He went to park the car."

"I am very sorry that I can't help you. It's not up to me," he said regretfully.

Demetrio returned and stood next to Cathy. "Hi," he said to the ticket seller. "What happened, Koukla? Everything okay?"

Cathy motioned him to be quiet. "Is there a chance someone might cancel their trip?" asked Cathy.

"That hardly ever happens, but it's not impossible. I'll put your name on the waiting list for the last trip out this evening. If there is a cancellation, you will be the first in line. What is your name?"

"Koukla. My name is Koukla."

The ticket seller furrowed his brow. "That's an unusual name," he said.

"My father is Greek. Koukla is a Greek name."

The ticket seller turned to his computer and punched away at his keyboard. After a moment, he looked at Cathy triumphantly. "You are very lucky," he said. "A couple from New York canceled two tickets for tomorrow night. Will that work?" Cathy looked at Demetrio, who nodded. "Yes, we'll take them," she said. The ticket-seller handed her the tickets and told them to be at the station the next evening no later than 6:00.

Cathy thanked the man and they turned away from the window. Cathy hugged Demetrio and jumped up and down with joy.

"Koukla, let's get some coffee here in the cafeteria."

"That's a good idea, Demetrio. We'll have a chance to enjoy this station – it was built back in the 1860s."

When they were seated in the cafeteria, Demetrio asked Cathy what she had scheduled next for them.

"First, we must find a place to sleep and then we'll see. Later, if you feel like it, we can go over to St. Joseph Proto-Cathedral. It's nearby here. It's a magnificent structure that was built in 1816. Bishop Benedict Joseph Flagot worked hard for five years to raise enough money to begin this building. It's Kentucky's first Catholic Church. We can see the beautiful stained glass windows, interesting icons and fine painting from Europe donated by Pope Leo XII, King Louis Phillips of France and others."

When they found a motel room, Demetrio hugged her and they fell together on the bed. He started kissing her. "First you have to let me take a shower," Cathy said, pushing him away playfully.

"I also need a bath," Demetrio said.

"Then let's take one together."

"I have no objections to that," Demetrio said, hopping up from the bed and walking to the bathroom, dropping his clothes along the way.

Later, as they lay in each other's arms, Cathy asked, "Demetrio, doesn't sex get you tired? I've never seen such endurance before."

"I am enchanted by your beauty, my princess. That's why I always want to be in your arms." Demetrio caressed and kissed Cathy softly, for a long while, until she drifted off to sleep. Then he closed his eyes and let his mind wander, hoping that sleep would find him.

It was all in vain, however. He was troubled by the fact that every time he made love with Cathy, he thought of Vanda. Not the happy Vanda of the old days, but a worried and sad Vanda, with a questioning expression on her face. "I must somehow go to Brazil," Demetrio thought. "The time has come for that." He glanced at Cathy lying next to him, and said to himself, "I will leave you, Cathy. Unfortunately I must leave you. You are young and beautiful. It will not be long before you find one other man who will offer you what I cannot." He leaned over and kissed her. Then he got up and showered again, got dressed, and sat by the window daydreaming, waiting for Cathy to wake up.

He thought of how different Kentucky was from the concrete jungle of Los Angeles, where only a few wealthy neighborhoods had trees and wide, open spaces. Here, looking out from his window, he could see the green of leaves and grass stretching out for miles.

Suddenly he remembered Konitsa. He desperately missed his family. He remembered his childhood friends, running along the gravel roads, playing with the rug ball, flying kites on the hill above the church next to the schoolhouse that stood at the edge of the village. He remembered his little sister Eleni and how he loved her. "What a curse it is to be away from your hometown," he whispered. His mind turned to Dora. He remembered her when she was just a young girl, playing in the schoolyard with her friends. She was so skinny and good-natured, always laughing, so simple and innocent. Then he remembered her as a grown woman, with his two children. "My children, where are my children?" he whispered, and hot tears rolled down his cheeks. He looked far into the clear sky. "Why, why? Why, God, did you punish me so severely?" He leaned his head on the wall and continued to cry. "What can I do to stop remembering? I wish I could cut out the part of my brain that remembers and throw it far into the ocean."

Cathy's voice interrupted his daydreaming. "Are you awake, Demetrio? What time is it, my love?"

Demetrio wiped his eyes and took a deep breath. "Two o'clock. Time has gone by very quickly."

"Come and hold me tight," she beckoned him from her bed. When he had settled next to her she said, "I think we'll only have time to visit the cathedral and walk around town. Tomorrow, we can visit My Old Kentucky State Home and then in the afternoon we'll take the dinner train."

"What are we going to see there?" Demetrio asked.

"Well, the guidebook says that in 1795 a judge named John Rowan built a house on 235 acres of land. Now the house and gardens with lots of trees, fragrant flowers, and wildlife, have been turned into a state park. The park got its name from the famous American folk song, 'My Old Kentucky Home," which was written by Stephen Collins Foster, who was Judge Rowan's cousin. Legend has it that Foster got inspired to write the song after one of his many visits to his cousin's estate. The song has become a kind of unofficial state anthem for Kentucky."

"Koukla, being with you, I'll learn all kinds of history." Cathy and Demetrio, visited St. Joseph proto-cathedral that evening and spent the rest of the day walking around town.

CHAPTER 14

The next morning, they headed out to Rowan's estate. The natural beauty of the area dumbfounded Demetrio. He was also enchanted by the 18th century costumes that the tour guides, guards, and other employees wore, and by the home's early American furnishings. Cathy and Demetrio spent an hour walking through the house, then they stepped outside, and strolled along the many shaded pathways that led them through the park.

At 5:00, they left for the train station. When they arrived, tourists were already lining up. An hour later, Demetrio and Cathy boarded the train and were ushered to their table, which they shared with an old couple from Lancaster, Pennsylvania. The inside of the boxcar was paneled in highly polished mahogany wood, and brass fixtures gleamed warmly in the dim light. The tables were draped in white linen cloths, and their dinner was served by men and women in 1940s period dress. Cathy and Demetrio couldn't help feeling like they had been pulled back in time to an age that was slow and unhurried.

The short two-hour ride, the beautiful, warm atmosphere perfumed with herbs and incense, the courteousness of the people who worked inside the restaurant, the period clothes they were wearing, and the distinctive decorations, enchanted everyone. Cathy thought this was one of the best experiences of her life. "I can see why my girlfriend said she wanted to get married many times just so she could come here for her honeymoons. Demetrio, I promise you that no matter how many times I get married, I will never come here again. I want this day here with you to remain with me for the rest of my life. I don't want to share what I feel this moment with anyone else." Then Cathy stopped and listened to the melody that came floating into the boxcar from the sound system. She took Demetrio's hands. Listen," she said. "That's Foster's song, *My Old Kentucky Home*." Cathy began humming along and tapped her hands softly to the beat of the music. "Demetrio, I only know the beginning and the end of the song. It goes like this:"

"The sun shines bright on the Old Kentucky Home,
'Tis summer, the Darkies are gay,
The corn top's ripe and the meadow's in the bloom
while the birds make music all day."

"No matter' twill never be light,
A few more days till we totter on the road,
then my Old Kentucky Home,
GoodNight!

"Very romantic, don't you think, Demetrio?"

He took her hands gently. "Yes, Cathy. Everything is very romantic today. Everything on this little trip is like a dream, far from reality –the train, the warmth of the place, the spring evening, and especially you. I will always remember this evening with you."

"Ah, you already forgot my name," Cathy said with a happy, glowing face. "My name is Koukla, not Cathy."

"No, Koukla, I did not forget it."

That night Cathy kept her body pressed close to his.

"I like you, Koukla," Demetrio said. "I like you a lot."

"I want to take advantage of all the time I am with you," Cathy replied. She took his hand and draped it over her waist.

"Hold me, Demetrio. I want you more than anything else in the world. I will remember you till the last breath of my life."

Demetrio lost himself in Cathy's arms that night, engaging in passionate lovemaking with no hesitation or bounds, complete and abundant. When Demetrio woke up in the morning, he carefully got up and went to the window. He lifted the shade slightly and realized that it was not yet fully dawn. He took a warm shower that he so badly needed. He felt tired, but in a good way. He felt pleased because he and Cathy were so well matched.

Demetrio dressed carefully so as not to wake Cathy, then slipped out of the room. He returned later carrying a plastic tray with their breakfast. He bent over and kissed Cathy on her forehead. "Wake up, Koukla. I brought breakfast," he said.

Cathy partly opened her eyes, stretched a few times and yawned. She reached out to touch him without saying a word. Demetrio hugged her and she put her arms around his neck and her warm cheek touched his.

"Did you sleep well, Koukla?"

Cathy smiled. "Did I sleep well? How could I not sleep well when all night I was in your arms? How well did you sleep?"

Demetrio loosened his arms to take a better look at her. "I slept better than a king. The beauty of my princess enchanted me."

Cathy embraced him again. "Let me take a quick shower and then I'll have my breakfast. Can you please hand me a large towel?"

Later as they sat at the small table, Cathy asked for the map. "I think it's in the car," Demetrio said. "I'll go bring it." He came back quickly. "Where do we go today?" he asked.

"I suggest we don't go anywhere today," Cathy said. "Let's stay here and rest. Tomorrow we can go to Hodgenville and from there to Cave City. Do you see here?" she asked pointing to the map. "This is Cave City. From there, it's about 115 miles to Cadiz, to the Land-Between-the-Lakes.

"People come thousands of miles to visit this place. We should go, too. Then we can decide what to do next. Maybe it would be a good idea before we return to Los Angeles to stop at Salt Lake City to meet my mom and dad. Besides, this was the original purpose of our trip. When we get to Cadiz, I'll call home to find out if my parents have returned."

"I am with you," agreed Demetrio, gently stroking her neck and shoulders.

Cathy turned to Demetrio. "And you, my love, are you having a good time vacationing with me?"

"My baby, do you have any doubt about that? Can't you see in my eyes that I am so pleased being with you?"

"Now, Demetrio, come close to me so I can tell you a little secret. Today we will sleep together again," she whispered. "I want you to love me just like last night."

Demetrio nodded.

The few days Demetrio had spent vacationing in Kentucky were enough to convince him that he had been wrong about America and its people. He realized that this was really the more genuine America. Even the local TV shows were different from those in Los Angeles. This trip was the ideal medicine for healing the wounds in his heart, which were still so fresh. Cathy's company and the beautiful surroundings contributed to a sort of rebirth for him. After talking with Cathy about Vanda and his child, Demetrio's hopes for starting a new family and a new life were renewed. Often he thought of Vanda. He wondered how her life was and how long she would wait for him.

Demetrio and Cathy spent the rest of the day touring the city. The only place they stopped to visit was Saint Joseph's Cathedral. Though they had planned to visit other tourist attractions, in the end they opted for seeing a bit of the city and its people instead. They stopped for drinks at a cafe and strolled around town eating ice cream, walking and hugging each other like two young lovers.

At one point Cathy smiled.

"Do you know what I said to the man at the ticket booth when I went to buy tickets for My Old Kentucky Diner Train?" she asked.

"Tell me, what did you say?"

"That we were newlyweds, married 10 days ago and on our honeymoon. I don't know why I said this."

Demetrio remained silent, and they continued walking side-by-side.

The following morning they started out for Hodgenville. As soon as they arrived, they went directly to the Lincoln Memorial, a huge structure built of marble and granite. Demetrio looked over the well manicured, tree-shaded lawns and admired the wonderful grounds. At the entrance to the Memorial stood six granite columns, with the words "WITH MALICE TOWARD NONE, WITH CHARITY FOR ALL," etched along the top of them.

"These wise words, Demetrio, are quoted from the man American people love and admire the most. He is like a father to all of us."

They went inside the Memorial and saw the long cabin in which Lincoln was born, and the bible Lincoln's father carried with him at all times.

When they left the memorial, it was already afternoon. They strolled under the tall trees enjoying the calmness of the surroundings. A light breeze was blowing, carrying along the scent of spring flowers and the sound of birdsong. Cathy and Demetrio walked silently holding hands. "What would you say if we stayed here tonight?" Cathy asked, breaking their long silence.

"It sounds like a good idea," replied Demetrio, "but now we should find something to eat because my stomach is making funny sounds."

"Demetrio, why don't you teach me more Greek? I'd love to know some, even if it's just a few words."

"Let's start right now," Demetrio replied. "SE AGAPO DASKALA MOU, which means, I love you, my teacher."

"You love me only as your teacher?" she asked.

Demetrio stood in front of her. "Cathy, I love you as a woman, and as a person, because you are an exceptional human being. Unfortunately, I cannot offer you any future. You know my situation."

Cathy bowed her head and a shiver ran through her. "For God's sake, Cathy, don't cry, Koukla, please don't cry," Demetrio pleaded.

But Cathy leaned against him, and continued to cry softly.

The night was sweet. A full moon shone in the vast, deep space of the heavens, surrounded by millions of stars that sparkled like fireflies. Demetrio commented that in Konitsa the word for fireflies means "ass fire." After some confusion, Cathy realized what he was saying and laughed.

"That's very good, very good. 'Ass fires' is more appropriate."

When they were back in the room alone, Cathy put her arms around Demetrio and kissed him passionately. "I want to take a shower with you," she said and kissed him again. "Tonight I want to sleep again in your arms."

"Me too, my princess. I want you. I want you close to me. My arms are open for you."

The next morning, they left for Cave City. Cathy navigated, reading the map and giving directions, while Demetrio drove. When they got there, they looked for a hotel and found one without too much difficulty, in spite of the many tourists. They dropped off their luggage, and went directly to Mammoth Cave. They had the option of going on one hour tour, or a three hour tour that took them deep inside the underground tunnels. Cathy thought for a moment, then said, "Demetrio, I would d really like to take the long tour but I have to confess, I am afraid to go so deep into the earth."

"Then we shouldn't even consider it," Demetrio replied, taking her in his arms. "Let's take the one-hour tour."

When they entered the cave, their guide told them the story of the maze of tunnels that formed the caverns.

"This part of the cave was discovered by white settlers about 1799. Findings of primitive tools, clothes, flintstones, and several naturally mummified bodies, indicate that people lived in here as far back as 4,000 years ago."

The ranger showed them how the early inhabitants made torches by soaking sticks in fuel and attaching them to the walls of the cave. Later explorers found their way with battery-powered lights clipped to hard hats. Then, in 1920, electricity was brought into the cave. "Those of you who want to experience the thrill of the old days of lighting," continued the ranger, "can take the Lantern Tour, a three-mile walk through the caverns which takes about three hours. There are 300 miles of caves below us that are connected by tunnels. This is the longest cave system in the world. It's more than 260 feet deep and the temperature is about 54 degrees throughout the year. For many years, the land where the caves are was privately owned but the government bought it up and it now belongs to all of us."

Demetrio was simply amazed. He was standing in the heart of a vast complex of underground tunnels, all of it the handiwork of nature. Cathy walked next to him holding his hand. "Demetrio, honey, I am cold," she said.

He rubbed her back hoping that the improved circulation would help. "A little while longer and we will be out of here, Koukla."

When they emerged from the cave it was 3:00 in the afternoon.

"What do you think of it, Koukla?"

Cathy took a deep breath. "Demetrio, I prefer nature on the outside with the sky, the trees and the birds."

Demetrio smiled. "To tell you the truth, I was thinking the same thing."

"Try to imagine, Demetrio, how life was in these caves 4,000 years ago."

Demetrio shook his head. "It's hard to imagine how people lived then. Personally I prefer to live at the present time."

"Demetrio, let's get something to eat. Somewhere around here is a fast-food place. Do you want to eat a hamburger? I am tired of eating in restaurants," Cathy said.

Demetrio immediately took her hand. "Let's go, Koukla. I am hungry as wolf."

Before returning to the City, they boarded a twin-diesel-powered cruiser for a tour of the nearby river. The banks were covered with lush vegetation, and the water was clear. Demetrio and Cathy tried to spot the deer, beavers, turtles and birds that lived along the river's banks. For Cathy and Demetrio, it was a perfect way to end the day.

When they arrived back at Cave City, they decided to take a walk before turning in for the night. "Everything is so romantic here, and you, Koukla, are so beautiful," Demetrio said. "All I want is to be with you."

Cathy smiled, happy with his compliment.

They left the car at the motel parking lot and began strolling.

"Demetrio, tomorrow we can spend our day at the national park in Cadiz. Let's go to bed early so we can start out first thing."

"I agree with you, Koukla."

"You know something, Demetrio? Vacationing is nice, we're having a great time together, but I miss our home. How about you?"

Demetrio did not answer. He stood there and gently caressed her face. Cathy took his hand and kissed it. "God," she thought, "I love Demetrio, I love him very much. I must be strong and fight the temptation."

Before long, they walked by a movie theater. Cathy stopped to read the posters in the window. "Demetrio, I've heard this film is pretty good. It's about immigrants, I think. Would you like to see it?"

"Let's go, Koukla, let's go my princess. I am no longer your king. I am just your slave."

Cathy hugged him. "I want you to always be my king and to take me in your arms as though I am your princess."

They went into the movie house and sat in a remote corner. Cathy lay in Demetrio's arms. When the movie was over, she turned to him. "Now, let's go to bed," she said as the lights came on around them.

Walking towards the motel, Cathy held Demetrio by the arm. "I want to take a shower with you," she said.

Demetrio smiled.

"Whatever you order, my princess."

CHAPTER 15

The days they spent together were ones of joy and happiness and the nights a sweet unending dream. Each of them tried to enjoy every moment of their time together, because they sensed that time was running out. Cathy knew well that as soon as they returned home to Los Angeles, Demetrio would start packing for Brazil.

The following day, they got up a little late and headed for the national park. As they walked deeper into the woods, Demetrio felt at peace. Walking with Cathy among the tall trees, the dense vegetation, and the colorful wildflowers, Demetrio felt he was in a magical forest.

"Koukla, all this time we have been together is just like a dream for me. To you I owe my return to life."

Cathy smiled. "Demetrio, don't exaggerate. If it hadn't been me, it would have been someone else. There is always someone on the riverbank waiting to throw us a safety line when we are drowning."

When they returned to town, they found a restaurant, then went for an after-dinner walk so they could enjoy the cool spring evening, the pleasant temperature and the quietness of the surroundings. Demetrio looked up and saw a myriad of stars sparkling in the clear sky. The night was quiet except for the chirping of crickets.

"How different life is here compared to the jungle of Los Angeles where we live," Demetrio commented.

"You are so right, honey. But don't forget that Los Angeles is a huge city where people have come from every corner of the world. Here, with a few exceptions, the people are locals."

That night Demetrio and Cathy slept quietly in each other's arms.

Early the next morning, Demetrio woke up with the first light of dawn. He got up and stood by the window, admiring the miracle of sunrise. He had never experienced such a view. The sun's disc was surrounded by a halo of brilliant colors as it crept above the mountaintop, painting the pale azure sky in golden pinks and lavenders. "Fucking nature," whispered Demetrio smiling.

A little later, they went down to the motel's dining room for breakfast. A young couple with their small child sat at a table nearby. Demetrio gazed at the child, suddenly remembering his own son. Cathy watched Demetrio silently. She reminded herself that he belonged to another woman, and to his son. For that reason she had to help reunite them. Yes, that was what she would do. She would gather up all her courage and accept Demetrio as a pleasant interlude in her life, as a beautiful but fleeting dream.

"Demetrio, we must get going."

Demetrio was somewhat startled. "Oh, yes. Yes. First, I have to go pay the bill, and then we leave. I'll drive today. Is that okay, Koukla?"

She smiled. "You drive half way and I'll drive the other half."

"How far is Cadiz?" asked Demetrio.

Cathy glanced at her watch. "It's 9:30. If we get going by 10:00, we'll be there in the afternoon."

A few minutes later, they were heading down Highway 65. Traffic was light, and they drove at a leisurely pace, enjoying the scenery. "Our vacation is almost over," Cathy said softly, looking out her window. Demetrio didn't know how to answer. He, too, dreaded their vacation coming to an end. Although he desired so much to hold his child in his arms and to see Vanda again, he felt a growing emptiness. He loved Cathy. With every passing day, her presence in his life grew vital. Demetrio had no doubt that without Costaki his love for Vanda would have by now slowly evaporated, and he would have been free to start his life anew with Cathy. Demetrio closed his eyes for a moment and imagined Vanda close to him. "God, please help me to make the right decision," he thought.

"You are daydreaming, Demetrio," Cathy said, interrupting his thoughts.

"Yes, I was thinking of what you said about our vacation coming to an end. It's something I hate to think about because spending these few days with you has been the most beautiful thing that could have ever happened to me. I love you, Koukla," he said deeply, pulling her close.

"I love you too, Demetrio, and I want to be with you always. But there is no way we can change our fate. We must take the paths that have been planned for us. It seems to me Demetrio that your path is leading Southward and mine Northward."

"Our fate?" Demetrio repeated angrily as though talking to himself. "Why must a person be so weak? Why must the most important decisions in his life be left to fate?"

"Unfortunately, that's how it is Demetrio. We must go our separate ways, and I believe this should happen soon. The longer we stay together, the harder and more painful our separation will become."

After a few moments, Cathy spoke. "Demetrio, slow down a bit and try to find a nice place to pull off so we can see the view better." Demetrio found a wide spot on the shoulder of the road and came to a stop. They got out of the car and looked around. A vast expanse of valley stretched out before them, dotted with trees, lush grass and scattered patches of wildflowers.

Cathy stretched, then turned to Demetrio, grabbed him by the hand, and with a laugh began running through the grass.

"Cathy, aren't you afraid of snakes?" Demetrio asked.

"I don't think there are snakes here," she replied. "But in case a venomous snake bites me, I want to die in your arms."

In a few seconds, they were quite far from the road. Cathy pulled Demetrio down by a large flowering bush. She grabbed him with both hands and kissed him. It was a hot kiss, full of passion. "I want you, Demetrio," she whispered.

Demetrio looked at her surprised. "Here?" he asked.

"Yes, here. It's the most romantic bed I have ever laid on."

Soon, they were lost in the joys of lovemaking. Then suddenly they heard a rustling noise from somewhere in the bush. The first thought that came to Cathy was that a snake was crawling nearby. The thought chilled the blood in her veins. Demetrio motioned to her not to move. For the next few moments, they both held their breath. Suddenly a well-fed, gray rabbit emerged, looking as surprised as Cathy and Demetrio, and nearly jumped over them as he scrambled for cover under a bush growing several feet away.

Demetrio held back his laughter and said sternly, "That rabbit has no manners at all!" Then he pulled Cathy back into his arms. They lay there, half-naked, looking into the clear, blue sky, listening to the birds chirping and the hum of cars from the highway.

Cathy got up slowly and started putting on her clothes. "Demetrio get up, it looks like we have company," she said looking towards the road. A patrol officer had pulled up and was walking around their car, peering inside the windows.

Holding hands, they returned quickly to the road. "Hi," Cathy said when they came close.

"Hi!" responded the patrolman, a tall, blond, well-built man with a rich, broad mustache. "Is everything all right?" he asked looking from Demetrio to Cathy.

"Yes, Officer. There is no problem. We just stopped for a short walk to stretch our legs," Cathy said.

"When we see a car stopped by the side of the road usually there's some kind of a problem."

"As I said, officer, we stopped for a rest."

"You went to rest in the bushes?" the policeman asked smiling.

"In the big city where we live, officer, there are no bushes or wild flowers. That's why we stopped here to take a short nature walk."

"Where do you live?" asked the policeman as he adjusted his sunglasses.

"We live in Los Angeles," responded Cathy immediately.

"In Los Angeles? What brings you here?"

"We are on vacation. That's all."

The policeman touched his chin and slightly lifted his wide brimmed hat. "Is the car yours?"

"No, it's rented. We rented it in Lexington where we are coming from."

"Who's the driver?"

"I am," Cathy responded, taking a step forward.

"May I please see your driver's license?"

Without replying, Cathy opened the car's door and pulled out her purse. "Here," she said handing him the license.

The officer looked at it for a moment. "May I please see the car registration certificate too?"

Irritated by all this, Cathy went back to the car and pulled an envelope from the glove compartment. "All the papers, including the rental agreement, are here," she said as she handed it to him.

"Please wait a moment. Don't get in the car," the officer said, turning back toward his vehicle.

Cathy could clearly hear the officer radioing the station, and became increasingly annoyed. Demetrio put his arms around her. "Don't get upset, Koukla. The officer is doing his job." Then he whispered in her ear, "Who knows what he saw to make him suspicious. So many arrests of outstanding criminals are made on routine traffic checks."

"But, Demetrio, can't he see, we are not the criminal type?"

"Don't be so upset, Koukla. Remember that sometimes innocent faces hide beastly criminals."

After a while, the officer returned and handed the car documents and driver's license to Cathy. "One last question," said the officer looking straight at Demetrio. "Do you have any opened liquor containers in your car?"

"No," replied Cathy dryly. "If you want, you can search the car."

"And the gentleman. Who is he?"

"He is my fiance."

"Your fiance does not speak English?"

"Sure he speaks English. Talk to him," Cathy said.

Looking at Demetrio, the officer asked, "Where are you from?"

"I am from Greece," Demetrio replied, looking the officer in the eye.

"Hm..." The officer smiled. "Your country is beautiful. A few years ago, my parents and a few of their friends went there to vacation at some of the islands and were very pleased. What is your name?"

"Demetrio Rendis."

"Welcome to Kentucky, Mr. Rendis. I Hope you both have a good time here. Sorry for the inconvenience."

Cathy smiled. "Thank you, officer. Thank you very much."

The officer touched his brimmed hat again, this time in a friendly greeting and left. Demetrio and Cathy got back in their car, and Cathy suggested to stop at Russelville, which was halfway to Cadiz.

"Whatever you say, Koukla," Demetrio replied. "We can stop at Russelville. I have no problem at all with that. Cathy let me say something else. I have seen so many beautiful places that if I see nothing more, I will still be very happy. The beautiful countryside around here is unbelievable. The vegetation, the trees, the flowers– I never expected to see so much of that here. Is Utah beautiful like this?"

"Demetrio, Utah is stunning. It is mostly desert with cliffs of red sandstone, deep canyons, and towering mountains." Cathy sighed. "I feel tired, Demetrio. Maybe you should just drive straight to Cadiz."

"Don't worry, Koukla. I can drive all the way to Los Angeles if you like. I just want you to be comfortable."

"You know, Demetrio, what happens to me? When I am away from my home, everything seems strange. It makes me tired. I miss especially sleeping in my own bed. If you were not with me, I would have a hard time falling asleep at night."

"Me too, Koukla. I have the same problem. When I lived in Konitsa, during school vacations I used to go with my sister to spend a few days at my uncle Spiro's house, swho lived in Ioannina, a beautiful city about 50 miles away from us. Ioannina is the provincial capital of our district. This city is built around a beautiful lake. The eels they catch in this lake are known all over the country for their delicious taste. Well, every time I went to uncle's house, I had a hard time sleeping. I felt always tired, while my sister slept like a rock. You know when I got over that? When I went in the army. That's where you learn a lot of new things that change your life. There I learned to sleep outside, on the ground. Many times the weather was cold and raining."

Demetrio continued to tell his story, softly lulling Cathy to sleep.

She woke up an hour later, just a few minutes before Demetrio brought the car to a stop in Russelville.

"We have arrived, Koukla," he said taking her hand.

Cathy glanced around her before getting out of the car to stretch her legs. "Let's go find a place to have some coffee," she said. "I need to throw some water on my face so I can wake up. Did I sleep long?"

Demetrio laughed. "Only one hour!"

They found a shop that sold donuts and coffee and sat at a small table, next to the window with a clear view of the road outside. "Russelville looks like a small place," said Demetrio.

" It's probably a little bigger than Cadiz, which has about 2,500 people," Cathy said.

"I love small places like this," said Demetrio. "You get to know everyone around you and you can have a lot of friends. I've lived in Los Angeles for so many years and still I don't have any friend. The people I know just say a plain 'Hi' and 'How are you today.' That's all."

"Life's pretty hard in the city, Demetrio. So many people can barely survive, and there's so much crime. It makes me scared for the children who live there, surrounded by gangs, drugs and prostitution. What about Greece? Is there social welfare? Does the government take care of young children that need help?"

Demetrio smiled, somewhat unprepared for the questions. "Cathy, I grew up in a poor, rural area. The people there are on their own. They work their farms and gardens to survive. I don't think there is any government support to speak of. At least not when I was young. Sometimes, to help someone who was really suffering, the mayor would go from house to house asking for donations of wheat or corn flour. In my school, there were kids who had no shoes, even during the winter. For decades, Greece was ruled by a few powerful, wealthy families who did as they wished. They controlled everything; they were like the Mafia. Most Greek people know what's going on, but there's not much they can do. For many years the Greek people have been asking, 'Why are there no young capable leaders?' The answer is simple – the system doesn't let anyone capable come to power. Those in control use terror, extortion and bribes to keep their privileged positions and keep reformers away. That's how the system works."

Cathy listened carefully. "It's so sad that these things are happening in Greece where civilization and democracy were born," she said.

"Unfortunately, that's how it is," replied Demetrio. " The Greek people have an obligation to work against the corruption and to try to rid the country of its oligarchy which is destroying us. Maybe now that Greece is part of the European Union things will improve."

"You want to hear my opinion, Demetrio? Greece is a small country which makes it easier for the powerful families to control all the key areas of politics and the economy."

"I don't agree with you, Cathy. There are other small European nations like Holland, Denmark, Norway, Switzerland, and others, that don't have anywhere near this level of chronic corruption."

"America is not perfect, either," Cathy said. "We have

more children living in poverty than any other nation in the western world. We are the richest nation on the planet and we can't take care of our kids. Can you fathom this, Demetrio? We have no social insurance, no guaranteed medical insurance, no child care centers available to everyone at minimal cost like they have in Europe. Congress just keeps ignoring the children. It's nonsense. America doesn't provide for its young, and then the kids grow up poor, uneducated and uncultured and the social ills of adulthood come back to haunt all of us."

"You, Koukla, should have gone into politics."

Cathy smiled. "Demetrio, we have a lot to say about politics and social welfare – unfortunately, nobody listens to us. I don't think the situation will improve, probably it will get worse in the future."

Cathy sipped her coffee and then looked at her watch. "Well, it's noon already, and I was hoping we'd be in Cadiz by now."

"Yes, but don't forget, we've had some unexpected, but lovely, delays", Demetrio said smiling.

"Yes, these are pleasant delays," Cathy said, caressing his hand softly. "Let's go on now Demetrio. I want to take a warm bath and rest a little."

CHAPTER 16

When they arrived in Cadiz, they drove to a motel that Cathy had picked from the guidebook. They checked in and when they got in the room, Cathy jumped on the sprawling bed. "Oh, Demetrio I'm so tired. But you know I just remembered that my parents must be back from Florida by now and I should call them. On our way home, we can stop by there so you can get a chance to meet them. We can stay there a few days before we fly back to Los Angeles."

"Sure I want to meet them, Koukla. I want to thank them very much for creating you, the best human being I have ever met."

"Thank you, Demetrio. It's very nice of you. I would have said the same thing to your parents because you are a fantastic person yourself. Now come sit next to me so we can figure out how far we are from my home. Maybe we'll drive there. What do you think?"

"Koukla, aren't you already tired from driving for so many days? I suggest we fly."

"Then let's fly," Cathy said and picked up the phone.

After a few rings, she heard her mother's voice. "Mother, it's me. How was your trip to Florida?"

"Cathy, how are you, sweetheart? The neighbor told us you came to see us. We just got back a couple of days ago. Where are you calling from?"

"I am in Kentucky, mother. In Cadiz, Kentucky."

"Are you by yourself?"

"No, Mom. I am with a very good friend. He is a wonderful man. His name is Demetrio. I am sure you'll like him when you meet him. He is very nice to me."

"Is he Russian?"

"No, Mom, he is Greek," Cathy said laughing. "What gave you the idea he is a Russian?"

"From the name. The name Demetrio sounds Russian. When are you going to be here?"

"In a few days, Mom, I'll call you back."

"Yes, my little Cathy. Call us and let us know."

"Mom, are you crying?"

"No, sweetheart. I just thought how beautiful it was when we all lived together and tears came to my eyes. You left and the house is empty. We are very lonely, sweetheart. Your Dad wants to talk to you, too. Stay on the phone for a minute so I can call him. He is out in the yard watering the flowers."

"Bye, Mom. I love you very much."

"Bye, my little girl. We'll be waiting for you."

Cathy's eyes watered and she tried hard to hold back her tears.

A few moments later, she heard her father's deep voice. "Cathy! How are you, my little girl? How is everything out there in Los Angeles?"

"I am not in Los Angeles, Dad. I am in Kentucky. I am okay. I miss you both a lot. How are you? Whatever happened with that pain in your knee, still hurting?"

"It's no big deal. The doctor thinks it's arthritis. But doctors don't always know everything, you know. They have to say something, even if it's a wild guess to show you they know. I am over 60 now and I still chop wood with an ax for the fireplace. Just like when I was 20."

"Dad, I am so happy to hear you are OK. I miss you, Dad."

"Your mother said you'll be here in a couple of days."

"I don't know yet. First I have to get the plane tickets. I'll call you back to let you know."

"Yes, sweetheart. Call back and let us know so we can pick you up at the airport."

"I love you, Dad."

"I love you too, my little princess. And think about moving back with us. There is no reason for you to live so far away."

Cathy was silent.

"Can you hear me, sweetheart?"

"Yes, dad. I can hear you. Bye now, and I'll call you when I get the tickets."

"Bye, honey. We'll be waiting for you."

Cathy hung up but couldn't lift her hand from the phone.

Demetrio got up from the bed and went next to her. "What's the problem, Koukla?" he asked.

Cathy smiled a bitter, sad smile. "There is no problem, Demetrio. Many times I think how strange human nature is. Not too long ago, I believed that I had an iron will and was very strong and self-assured. Now I wonder about myself. Things that at one time didn't bother me, now I feel very strongly about."

"What do you mean? What are these things you are talking about?" asked Demetrio.

"Well, like love affairs, family, children... these kinds of things. Now I am thinking about what my father said and I'm beginning to believe he is right. Why should I live alone, far from home? Before, I never cared if this bothered my parents. All that mattered to me was that I felt good with what I was doing."

"Come on, Koukla. All of us make mistakes in our life. But remember, it's never too late," Demetrio said giving her a hug.

Cathy nodded. “Yes, you are right. It’s never too late. Maybe there is still time to correct some of my past mistakes. For now though, I have to take care of the airplane tickets. Then we’ll see.”

Cathy got on the phone and soon had reserved two tickets for Utah. Then she called her parents to let them know that they would be arriving the day after tomorrow.

While Cathy was on the phone, the idea came to Demetrio to call his uncle. Demetrio had finally come to realize that he couldn’t blame his misfortunes on Christo, and it was time to make amends. When Cathy hung up with her parents, Demetrio made his call.

“Hello,” Christo’s voice came through the line loud and clear.

“Uncle, it’s me, Demetrio.”

“Demetrio...! Where have you been, son? Why didn’t you call me? I’ve been looking all over for you. Are you okay?”

“Yes, uncle. Now I am okay. How about you? Have you heard anything from Eleni?”

“Demetrio, I have so many things to tell you. We have to meet right away. Eleni is expecting me in Konitsa to get her and bring her here to America. I promised her that as soon as I find out anything about you, I’d call. Eleni is in bad shape. Whenever I call her, she is constantly crying. She wants to talk to you real bad. She is concerned something bad happened to you.”

“Thank you, Uncle, thank you for everything.”

“ Now... where are you, Nephew? Are you here in Los Angeles?”

“No, Uncle. I am in Kentucky.”

“Kentucky? How did you get there?”

“I’ll tell you all about it, Uncle, when we get together. In any case, don’t worry about me. Now I am much better.”

"When are you coming back to L.A.? "

"I think in about a week. As soon as I get there, I'll call you to let you know."

"Please, Demetrio, call me right away, I want to see you." Christo's voice broke for a moment. "What happened was real awful. Who would have thought of something like that happening? I've been sick since then. I'm coming and going to doctors and hospitals. I thought I was going to die from the shock." Christo now was crying out loud.

"Uncle... Are you okay?"

"I am okay, son. After talking to you I feel a lot better."

"I understand, Uncle, how you feel. Those horrible days were a nightmare for me, too. I felt like killing myself."

"Demetrio, I want to tell you something else. I made out my will and left you as my beneficiary. I want you to know, if something happens to me, you get complete control of my estate."

"Uncle, don't say these things. Nothing is going to happen to you. Just take care of yourself and watch your health. I have decided to go to Brazil to be with Vanda and my child. I am not going to stay long in America."

"Demetrio, you can do whatever you want. The decision about my will is mine. I have contacted also Costa, the carpenter. Vanda gave me his address. There are lots of letters from Vanda for you. I talked to Vanda many times. The poor girl is worried to death about you. When she found out about the tragedy, she was calling just about every day trying to find out what happened to you."

Demetrio's heart swelled with love and sympathy for his uncle.

"Demetrio?"

"Yes, Uncle?"

"Listen to me carefully. I gave Costa a sealed envelope.

It's from my lawyer. Inside the envelope are all the instructions about my will."

"Come on, Uncle. Please, stop talking about wills. I hope you live to be over 100. Good bye now and I'll see you soon when I get to Los Angeles. Okay?"

"Yes, son. When you get here, we'll talk about it. But try to get here quickly."

"Bye, Uncle, and take care of yourself."

"Good bye, Nephew. I really appreciate your call. I feel so much better now. Bye son."

"My poor uncle," whispered Demetrio after he hung up. "He was really hit hard by my misfortune. I feel so bad now for the way I treated him and what I thought of him."

"Just take it easy, Demetrio. I can understand how hard it was what you went through. I am sure it is still hard for you. Psychological trauma of this magnitude takes a long time to heal. Now, don't you think it would be a good idea to go out for a walk and then later go have dinner?" Then Cathy brought her face close to Demetrio's and touched her nose to his.

On they way out, they asked the clerk at the registration desk where they could find a good restaurant. "You can go to the Kentucky Smokehouse, but remember, it closes at 8:30. If you decide to go there for dinner, you should call to make reservations. I can give you the number," the clerk said. They went for a walk, and returned to their room a short time later. "Cadiz, Cathy, reminds me very much of my home town. Somehow I have the impression that this place is about the same size as Konitsa."

Cathy stood behind him and circled her arms around his waist. Demetrio pulled her arms closer. "Just stay with me like this for a little while," he said. "I like it when you are so close to me." Then he turned and kissed her.

Cathy fell in his arms.

Demetrio lifted her up and placed her softly on the bed. He kissed her hungrily while he helped her undress.

Cathy pulled him on top of her and kissed him passionately.

Later that evening, they went to the Smokehouse Restaurant. The wine was so tasty that one bottle followed the next in quick succession. The wine went straight to Cathy's head, and she laughed easily like a child. When they walked out, she hung onto Demetrio's neck and sang a tune softly. "I feel so happy, Demetrio. And I owe it to you. You gave me these feelings. Now I realize what it means to be happy." Then, laughing, she continued, "Demetrio, I'll tell you a joke. I know lots of them. You want to hear one?"

Demetrio kissed her. "I love to see you happy like this, Koukla. You make me forget all my problems. Come now, tell me the joke."

Cathy thought for a moment, scratched her head a little and said, "A man had a parakeet that spoke almost like a human being. The bad thing about it was that it knew a lot of swear words. The bird's name was Miko. The neighbors frequently complained to the owner because of the swearing. When the situation became unbearable, the parakeet owner took it by the neck and threw it in the chicken coop for punishment. When Miko found himself among hens and roosters, he trembled fearfully and went to a corner of the coop where he tried be as inconspicuous as possible. A couple of roosters started arguing over which one of them would rule the roost. Not able to come to an agreement, they started a fistfight. To make peace, Miko went up to them and asked them graciously to stop fighting. The two roosters decided to get rid of the parakeet first and then resolve their differences. So they beat up poor Miko so badly that he fell down with his legs up and not one feather on his body. In the afternoon, when the man went to get his parakeet, he saw it lying on the floor. 'What happened to you, Miko?' Miko pointed to the two roosters standing at corner of the coop. 'Boss, those two made me very angry, and when I get mad and I get my jacket off, nobody can stop me."

Cathy turned to look at Demetrio, "Did you like it, or was it too long?"

"Yes, it was good. I like jokes."

"Now I am going to tell you a shorter one," said Cathy. "The flea was making love to the female elephant. At one point, the elephant lifted her trumpet and trumpeted with all her might, 'Did I hurt you, sweetheart?' asked the flea."

Demetrio laughed heartily. "Koukla, tonight you are so nice. You are the most beautiful woman in the world." A little while later they returned to the motel with Demetrio driving the car clumsily. Fortunately, there was hardly any traffic on the roads and the distance was relatively short.

They spent the following day at the Barkley Resort Park. It is a vast verdant area of 3,700 acres between Lake Barkley and Lake Kentucky. This place is a truly magnificent sight, not only for the visitors but also for the natives as well who may spend there a pleasant weekend with their families. Everything there is well organized, and very clean. The lake has a swimming beach and provides facilities for boating and fishing, backpacking, basketball, picnicking and restaurants.

"Demetrio, let's go for some horseback riding." Cathy said.

Holding hands, they continued walking till they reached the place where they rent horses. Within a few minutes, they were riding under the giant trees. Cathy turned to look at Demetrio next to her. "Do you feel nature's fragrance?" asked Cathy.

"I feel great. This vacation was very good for both of us. We gave our poor lungs the chance to breathe a little clean air. And most importantly, we got the chance to get to know each other better. Don't you think so?"

"That's exactly right, Demetrio, we got the chance to know each other a lot better."

"Cathy, can we gallop a little?"

"I'd love that, but it is not allowed. The ranger explained this to me when we picked up the horses."

When they returned the horses, they rented a boat and went for a very romantic boat ride in the lake. After that, they continued walking in the park passing through amazing parts of vegetation and flowers. "It drives me crazy when I think we are going back to Los Angeles," said Cathy.

Not knowing what to say, Demetrio remained silent. Maybe because he knew his stay in Los Angeles was going to be a short one. "What time will we get going tomorrow for Paducah?" he asked avoiding a direct response to her comment.

"Paducah, Demetrio, is about 60 miles from Cadiz. The plane for Salt Lake City leaves at 5:30 in the afternoon so we'll have plenty of time, no matter what time we leave in the morning."

They returned to the motel in the afternoon and didn't come out again. "Demetrio, I feel tired," Cathy said coming out of the shower. "We did plenty for today."

Around 10:00 the following morning, Cathy and Demetrio were heading for Paducah. The road traffic was relatively light, which allowed Cathy who was driving to pick up speed. When they were nearing the town Eddyville, they heard police sirens. Cathy looked in the rear view mirror and saw a patrol car right behind her with its lights blinking. Cathy slowed down and moved to the side of the road.

"Hi," said the officer courteously when he came by the side of her still-closed car door.

"Hi," answered Cathy, making an effort to hide her nervous smile. "What's going on officer?"

"Speed limit," he answered immediately.

Cathy didn't say another word, knowing that the best strategy she could follow at the moment was to be polite.

"Can I see your driver's license and the car registration?"

"It's a rental car," Cathy said, as she handed him her driver's license.

The officer bent down threw to glance inside the car and took a questioning look at Demetrio. Then he walked away towards the patrol car.

Demetrio took Cathy's hand. "Don't worry, Koukla. The most he can do is give us a ticket. You never know, he may even let us go."

"Demetrio, I suspect we are not going to get away without a ticket this time." Pointing to the officer she continued, "He is the kind of guy who would give a violation to his own father if he caught him doing something illegal. Maybe, Demetrio, this is the proper thing to do because it's the only way to keep law and order."

In a moment, the officer returned, gave her back her driver's license and the ticket to sign.

Cathy took the ticket and thanked the officer.

"Miss Morrison, have a nice day and drive safely," said the officer. "It's a shame to endanger your young life."

A little while later, Cathy was again driving the car on the well-paved highway. "I see you are daydreaming," said Demetrio. "Didn't we agree not to worry about little things?"

"I am not worried so much about the ticket," Cathy said. "I am worried about the insurance company. I know very well that I live in a country with laws which must be obeyed by its citizens if we want to have some form of democracy—and I am proud of living in such a country."

Demetrio smiled. "Why do you say 'some form of democracy?'"

"No matter how you cut it, democracy favors the financially stronger – or to put it another way, 'money talks' as we say in America. But even this less-than-100-percent democracy is better than what they have in other countries. Just imagine, Demetrio, if what happens in many other places, where you give a small bribe to a policeman to look the other way and he curtsies to you like a slave, also happened here. Demetrio, let's come back to reality now. In five more minutes we will be in the city of Eddyville. Do want to make a short stop?"

"Yes, Koukla. Let's make a stop. In any case, we have to change seats because I'll be driving from here to Paducah. Okay, Koukla?"

"Yes, my love, whatever you command, my Greek prince."

"That was nice," said Demetrio laughing. "The Greek prince who captured the heart of the beautiful American girl. Nice town," continued Demetrio as they reached Paducah.

"Paducah, Demetrio, is a city of 27,000 souls. It was officially founded on 1827. Here one can enjoy fantastically green scenery that is due to the plentiful waters from the two large rivers, the Ohio and the Tennessee, which converge nearby. These two rivers contribute to the prosperity of this area, and to disasters as well due to frequent flooding. The biggest disaster occurred in 1937 when the whole area around here became a huge lake."

Demetrio bent and kissed her. "My sweet teacher," he said touching her face gently.

Cathy took his hand for a moment. "Demetrio, I think we should first go to the airport to check in, then return the car to the rental company."

They returned to the airport at 4:00 in the afternoon and sat at a table in the airport cafeteria to have a quick meal. "Our vacation is over," said Cathy with a sad tone to her voice. "Everything resembles a sweet dream."

Demetrio got up and went to sit next to her. "Koukla," he said as he rested his arm on her shoulder. "Come now, I want to always remember you happy with a smile in your face."

Cathy just shook her head. "I'll try Demetrio, I'll try not to be sad. Perhaps, the day will come when my heart will be happy again."

The plane took off without delay and within a few minutes they were flying. Objects on the ground receded as the plane altitude increased. Cathy lay her in Demetrio's arms and held on to his hands.

After about an hour, the airplane landed at the International Airport in St. Louis, Missouri, where more passengers came on board. Half an hour later they were flying again. "Soon I am going to see my parents again," Cathy said. "I've missed them so much. Many times I remember the games I played with my dad when I was a young girl. Our house, Demetrio, is built on a large lot, as are all the other houses in our neighborhood. In our backyard, there is a small pond with ducks. At first, my dad bought a pair of ducks and gradually they multiplied. I loved to watch the little ducklings swim next to their mother, one after the other, linedup like tiny soldiers. Later on, he bought a pair of geese too. You should have seen, Demetrio, what happened with the geese. They'd run after me and chase me until I'd stop to give them food. Those times were beautiful," whispered Cathy. "But they passed too quickly." Then she turned her head to look out of the small aircraft window. A little later, she rested her head on Demetrio's shoulder and fell asleep.

It was now dark and the lights inside the plane cabin were turned on. The voice of the stewardess, telling the passengers that they would be landing in a few minutes at Salt Lake City International Airport, woke Demetrio up. Cathy was still asleep. "Koukla, we have arrived," he said as he kissed her.

Cathy opened her eyes. “Wow, I’ve been sleeping for over two hours,” she said after looking at her watch. “How about you Demetrio? Did you sleep at all?”

“Oh, yes, I slept, too. I just woke up.”

CHAPTER 17

The airplane landed at the airport smoothly. Once in the terminal, Cathy stopped and glanced around her. "Cathy!" yelled a woman's voice from across the way. Demetrio looked up and saw a middle-aged woman with open arms running towards them. She was followed by a man a few steps behind. Cathy dropped her small suitcase and rushed towards them.

"Mom... Dad..." Cathy yelled happily and fell into her parents' arms. Demetrio stood there, pensively watching.

Cathy drew back from her parents' embrace and took Demetrio by the hand. "Dad, this is Demetrio," she said smiling. The man extended his hand and said warmly, "My name is Robert Morrison. Welcome, Demetrio."

"My pleasure," Demetrio replied.

"Mother, meet Demetrio," Cathy said. "And remember he is Greek."

Mrs. Morrison went up to him, hugged and kissed him. "Welcome, son," she said. Cathy's mother put Demetrio instantly at ease. She had a pleasant disposition and a ready smile. Cathy's father was a large man with broad shoulders, a well-combed beard and a well-trimmed, broad mustache. His daughter had inherited his sparkling blue eyes.

They gathered their bags and quickly drove the short distance home. The evening was cool and clear, the moon and stars shining brightly. Cathy's house was one of several that stood on the block, each surrounded by a white picket fence. That night, Cathy's father grilled the best steaks Demetrio had ever tasted, as her mother prepared the rest of a memorable feast. When, at last, they were ready for bed, it was well past midnight.

Demetrio slept in the guest bedroom next to the kitchen. He was exhausted and had no trouble falling asleep. A few hours later, he awoke to soft hands gently caressing his face. He opened his eyes and through the darkness saw Cathy sitting close to him, smiling.

"I can't fall asleep," she said kissing him. "I was thinking of you."

Demetrio hugged her. "What will happen if your father or mother wake up?"

Cathy reassured him. "They are heavy sleepers, both of them. They only wake up in the morning. Besides, we are not going to make a lot of noise. Okay, darling?" With a quick movement, Cathy threw off her robe and nestled in beside him.

Demetrio hugged her tightly. "Koukla, my sweetheart," he said, his voice trembling.

"You have spoiled me and I no longer can sleep alone," Cathy said quietly. Then she began to kiss him slowly, working her way down the length of his body, whispering words he couldn't and didn't need to fully hear. He felt Cathy's body burn strangely and felt his own body respond with the sweet shiver of passion. They made love joyfully, and then Cathy drifted off to sleep in Demetrio's arms. It was a soft sleep, light as a feather, sweet and pleasant.

When she woke up a few hours later, she turned to see Demetrio sleeping peacefully by her side. In the semi-darkness, she made out the handsome contours of his face, relaxed now, like a happy and satisfied child. Suddenly, Cathy was overcome by a tranquillity that filled her soul. She was satisfied with herself for having rescued Demetrio from the dark abyss into which fate had thrown him, and she was glad that she had been able to guide him back to life and hope. Cathy gazed at Demetrio a few moments longer. Then she quietly slipped back to her room.

With the first light of dawn, the rooster crowed, waking Demetrio. He lay in bed for a few seconds, staring at the ceiling, not quite sure where he was. Then he remembered that he was in Cathy's parents' house, and that she had crept into his room last night and had slept with him. He felt the crumpled sheets with his hands to make sure she was no longer there. He felt somewhat relieved because under no circumstances did he want to cause any friction with her parents. He yawned a few times and before he knew it, he fell back to sleep again.

When Cathy woke up that morning, she went directly to the window. From there she had a good view of the garden, with the flowerbeds and the pond. She recalled her happy childhood days of playing around the water's edge, feeding the ducks, and trying to run away from the hissing geese. Slowly, she counted the years that had passed since she had first moved away from home. Five years! Five wasted years. Now that she was back at home with her family she kept wondering why she had ever left. She realized that in those five years she had grown. She no longer felt the need to prove to her parents that she could stand on her own. She felt that those five years away from home had been an awful mistake.

Cathy took a hot bath, then went downstairs. In the kitchen, she found her mother seated at the table next to the window. She went up to her and kissed her. "Good morning, Mom."

"Good morning, Cathy. How did you sleep?"

"Very well, Mom. I had the best sleep ever."

"Come, have a cup of coffee. When Demetrio gets up, I'll prepare your favorite breakfast."

"Thank you, Mom. I am so happy to be back here with you again."

"Cathy, you know this home is yours. We always wait for you."

"Thank you, Mom. You are so nice to me. I am going to do that. First, I have to complete a job I am doing."

"What kind of job is it? Will it going to take long?"

"The job is with Demetrio. Mom, I want to talk to you about that." She paused. "Is Dad gone?"

"Oh, yes. Your Dad leaves quite early every day. He'll be back around four. Now come close and talk to me."

They began talking at the kitchen table, then moved out into the garden. Cathy told her mother Demetrio's life story and how his problems affected her own life.

Cathy's mother held her daughter's hands and listened carefully. At one point, Cathy began to cry. "I love Demetrio, Mom. I love him so much. I don't know what to do. I feel I'll die if he leaves me." She leaned into her mother's arms, sobbing as her mom quietly stroked her hair.

"Oh, my little Cathy, my baby," her mother said with sadness. "It is a difficult situation, and one that you have to figure out for yourself. No one can tell you what you should do. But I can try and give you some advice. You must turn your heart to stone and forget Demetrio. No matter how much you love him, you will never make him truly yours. He is connected to another woman, and to his son — especially to his son. Even if he stays with you, his mind will always be in Brazil. And you must always remember to never believe everything men tell you."

Cathy immediately pulled away from her mother. "Mom, Demetrio is not an ordinary man. I am sure of this. He has always been honest with me from the first moment we met. He never took advantage of the situation. I absolutely believe that

Demetrio is a serious man, with genuine feelings and with a lot of integrity. That's what made me love him."

"What else can I say, sweetheart? I just hope that things turn out best for both of you. You are both young and I am sure you'll solve your problems. Remember, Cathy, life is generous. It always gives us a second chance."

It was 9:00 when Demetrio woke up again. He got out of bed, took a nice hot bath and went out of his room. He listened carefully, but no one else seemed to be in the house. It was quiet, as quiet as the inside of an empty church. He walked to the kitchen but still saw no one. Then he stepped out of the rear kitchen door into the backyard and was amazed by the view. The garden was artfully landscaped with a profusion of flowers and a well-manicured lawn. Trees lined the property and a pond glimmered in the sunlight. Ducks swam to and fro, diving for treats and fanning their wings. A large white goose strutted proudly back and forth, and Demetrio spontaneously laughed because he recalled the story Cathy told him about the geese chasing her for the food. Then he spotted Cathy and her mother sitting on a wooden bench.

When Cathy saw him, she got up and ran to him. "Good morning, Demetrio. Come sit with us," she said taking him by the hand.

"Good morning, Mrs. Morrison," Demetrio said when he got close to her.

"Good morning, Demetrio. How did sleep?"

"Fine, Mrs. Morrison. The bed was really comfortable and I was so tired, I slept like a log."

Cathy's mother got up. "You kids stay here. I'll go make your breakfast and I'll call you when it's ready," she said heading towards the kitchen door.

Cathy held Demetrio's hand. "Come, let's take a walk until breakfast is ready," she said.

"Is your father inside?" Demetrio asked.

"No, he leaves early in the morning for work," Cathy answered. "He manages a local bank. He's worked there ever since he got out of college, more than 30 years."

They continued along until they reached the far end of the garden. Behind a large fenced-in area were two deer. Cathy opened the gate, went inside, and began petting the animals. Chickens scattered, pecking at the ground with their beaks.

"What do you think of my house?" Cathy asked.

Demetrio shook his head in wonderment. "What can I say, Koukla? This is not an ordinary house. It's like a mansion. All these trees and flowers that are here, and all well groomed, reminds me of gardens of a rich palace of the old days."

Cathy smiled. "Just wait, Demetrio, until you see the homes of the truly rich. They are 10 times bigger than our house."

"Tell me something, Cathy. Who takes care of all of these grounds?"

"The gardener comes once a week. My father does most of the work on weekends. It's his hobby."

"From what I see, your father must not have any free time for anything else."

"Oh, no," replied Cathy. "My father is very active. He bowls and golfs and finds time for other things – and he's good at what he does. When I was a little girl, he taught me how to bowl. I used to play in the women's league when I lived here. Even though I played for many years, I never got as good as him."

"To tell you the truth, Koukla, I know nothing about bowling. I have never even been inside a bowling alley."

"Then we have to go someday," Cathy said. "I am sure you'll love it. If you like, we can go one night when my father is competing so you can see him in action."

Suddenly Cathy's mother called from the kitchen door. "Cathy, Demetrio, come in, breakfast is ready."

The three of them sat down at the kitchen table to a sumptuous breakfast of fried eggs, sausages, toast and cheese.

"Mrs. Morrison, this is a full meal," commented Demetrio.

She smiled. "It's no big deal, Demetrio. It's a normal breakfast. Cathy, where do you plan to go today?"

"We hadn't really thought about it, Mom," Cathy said, looking at Demetrio.

"Why don't you go to Temple Square?" Cathy's mother suggested. "Maybe you can take a tour of the Tabernacle."

Cathy clapped her hands with enthusiasm. "That's a great idea, Mom. The Tabernacle, Demetrio, was built by the Mormons in 1867," she explained. "Just imagine – its dome is 150 feet wide and 250 feet long and is self-supporting. It was designed by an engineer named Henry Grow who was famous for his bridges. Inside is the Tabernacle Organ - famous for its twelve thousand pipes," Cathy continued. "The tabernacle itself is known for its acoustics – if a coin drops at one end of the great hall, it can be heard at the other end 170 feet away. Since 1932, CBS has been broadcasting the Sunday morning services. To this day, the choir tours in North America, Europe and Japan."

"Your daughter, Mrs. Morrison, is a terrific teacher," said Demetrio. "She knows everything and in great detail. In our short tour when we visited her uncle in Lexington, she told me the whole history of Kentucky."

"Demetrio, because she is my daughter I don't want to brag about her, but Cathy is very intelligent. We wanted her to be a teacher and stay close to us. She is very capable and could have easily accomplished this but she decided to study computers and live alone, like an orphan, in Los Angeles –

as if there are no jobs around here." Suddenly, Cathy's mother looked sad. "Let's hope God leads her back to her home," she said. Then she took off her glasses and dabbed a tissue at the corner of her eyes.

"Come on, now Mom. Please, don't start complaining again," Cathy said.

Cathy's mother got up and stood by the window overlooking the garden. Demetrio followed her with his eyes and could see that she was crying. Cathy got up and went next to her. Within moments, mother and daughter were crying in each other's arms.

Demetrio left the kitchen, and began walking under the trees that graced the yard. He wondered why Cathy, an educated and intelligent young woman with everything anyone might desire, chose to leave home to pursue an uncertain future in a city as chaotic and dangerous as Los Angeles. A little later, Cathy found Demetrio sitting on a wooden bench at the far end of the garden.

"I left you all alone," Cathy said, kissing him lightly on the lips.

"I am not alone. The trees are full of birds, and the earth is full of small animals that keep me company," he said. "Do you know that a moment ago I saw a turtle?"

"Demetrio, if you look along the edge, near the fence, you will find some more turtles, and in the bushes you will find porcupines," Cathy said. Then she looked at her watch. "It's almost 11:00. Do you want to go visit Temple Square and take a tour of the Tabernacle?" she asked. "Later, if we feel like it, we can go somewhere else. My mother lent me her car," Cathy added, twirling the keys around her fingers.

That day, besides the Tabernacle, Demetrio saw the beautiful Temple built in 1893, which also belongs to the Mormons. "The majority of the population of Utah, Demetrio, including my own family, are Mormons," Cathy said. " I was baptized in this Temple. Only children of Mormons are allowed to be baptized or married here. I don't know if this is called discrimination," said Cathy laughing. "Before we return home, Demetrio, we'll take a ride by the university. I went to school there, too. It's not far from here. It is a large campus with beautiful buildings. It's filled with plenty of trees and green lawns."

When they arrived, Cathy parked the car, and the two of them began strolling through the sprawling campus, stopping at some of the more prominent buildings. They visited the recreation center, the theater, the stadium, and some classroom buildings. Demetrio was simply stunned. "Koukla, this is just like a city by itself," he said with amazement. They continued on their way, stopping in front of a huge swimming pool.

Sadenldy, Cathy took his hand and said happily, "I want to tell you something, Demetrio."

Smiling, Demetrio stopped in front of her. "When I see you happy like this I know I am going to hear something good."

"It's my birthday Saturday. Both my mother and father asked me to stay a few extra days and leave next week so we can all celebrate together. They want to have a party and invite some friends and relatives."

Demetrio lifted Cathy in his arms and spun her around. "Happy birthday, Koukla. With all my heart I wish you happiness forever. Sure we can stay as many days as you like. Nobody is pressuring us to go back to Los Angeles."

Cathy cuddled up against him. "Demetrio, you are so nice to me, how I wish things were different."

Later, when they returned home, they found Cathy's mother in the kitchen preparing dinner.

"What wonderful feast are you preparing for dinner, Mom?"

"Baked chicken with potatoes and salad. It's something all of us like. I hope Demetrio likes it, too."

"Mrs. Morrison, I don't think there is any food I don't like," Demetrio answered.

"Demetrio, how long have you been in America?" Cathy's mother asked.

"It's nine years now," he replied smiling.

"Well, I want to congratulate you for speaking such good English."

"I am trying, Mrs. Morrison. When I first came, I went to night school for quite a while. This helped me a lot. I was fortunate to have a very conscientious teacher. Now I have the very valuable help of your daughter. When I make a mistake, she corrects me."

Cathy laughed. "Demetrio is an excellent student Mom. And what is most important is he wants to learn." Cathy peeked in the oven door. "Mmmm..." she breathed in deeply. "Mom, your cooking smells so delicious."

"Cathy, take Demetrio and go out into the garden now. It's a pleasant evening and you shouldn't be spending it indoors. Your father will be home any minute now and I need to finish setting the table."

"Let me help you, Mom," Cathy said eagerly.

"No, sweetheart. I don't need any help. I've got plenty of time to do it by myself."

Demetrio and Cathy wandered into the garden. "Your mother is such a nice person," Demetrio said.

"My father is good, too," Cathy replied. "I'm so lucky to have such wonderful parents – but I've caused them so much grief. They begged me with tears in their eyes not to leave home but I didn't pay any attention. I was looking for freedom. I wanted to leave Salt Lake behind and go to a big city, to see the skyscrapers and the freeways, the beaches, the excitement. I was so jealous of people who actually got to live in such places.

"But then I moved to Los Angeles, and I began to realize that life in the big city was hard – people were indifferent, the beaches were smelly and polluted, everyone was too busy running from one thing to another to ever stop and really enjoy anything." Cathy paused for a moment. "I even dreamed of becoming a Hollywood actress," she continued, shaking her head ruefully. "When I was in college, people would tell me I looked like Marilyn Monroe. When I got to Los Angeles, I looked up a man through a newspaper ad who promised me miracles. He said he knew all the hot shot movie directors and that he could make me famous. The first day I met him in his office on Hollywood Boulevard, he asked me about my background and my personal life – if I lived alone, where my hometown was, and if I had a boyfriend. The whole time we talked, he held on to my hand. He asked me to have dinner with him that night to seal our deal. During dinner he invited me to go see his Century City condominium. Naturally, I refused, and he got very upset. Despite all this, he promised that he would call to introduce me to his friend who was a producer of commercials. 'All the big stars of Hollywood started out in commercials,' he told me when he dropped me off at my apartment. I am still waiting for his phone call."

Demetrio listened silently. He had heard many such stories about the famous Hollywood. "Cathy, tell me something, why didn't you drop everything and go back home?" Demetrio asked.

"I was embarrassed," she replied quickly. "I didn't want my parents to think I couldn't make it on my own. That's the reason I didn't go back, Demetrio. Now I realize how wrong I was. Now I know that my poor parents love me very much and want me to be with them."

Demetrio reached for Cathy's hands. "Koukla, it's never too late. It's not a bad idea to come back to your home. Look at me and promise me that you will try."

"I am sure I will come home, Demetrio," Cathy replied.

"That's good. I am convinced that the proper place for you is right here and not back in Los Angeles."

Suddenly, Cathy's father called from the kitchen door, his deep voice booming across the garden. "Hi, I am home."

Cathy ran up to him. "How was your day today, Daddy?"

"Just like every other day, sweetheart. Working at the bank is very boring. Nothing changes from day to day. And how was your day?"

"We visited the Tabernacle, and after that the University."

By now, Demetrio had come near them. "Good evening, Mr. Morrison," he said.

"Good evening, Demetrio."

"Dad, Demetrio wants to learn to bowl," Cathy announced. "Can we come with you Friday?"

"Sure you can. It should be exciting – two teams are tied for first place. My daughter can teach you, Demetrio She is a good bowler. Do you play any sport, Demetrio?"

"Not now. When I was young back in my country I used to play soccer, and while in the army I played for the National Armed Services Team. If I had not injured my knee, I could have probably become a professional soccer player. I wanted that very much, and I think I was qualified. Unfortunately, fate leads every person according to its own wishes and does not care what we want."

"What you just said Demetrio is very true."

By now all three of them had entered the kitchen where Cathy's mother was setting the table. "I am going for a quick shower and I'll be back," said Mr. Morrison as he climbed the stairs.

Later, when they were all seated at the table, Cathy's father led them in prayer. Demetrio was once again reminded of his own family. Every time they sat down at the table to eat, his father would pray, thanking God for providing the goods for their dinner table. Then he would make the sign of the cross over the bread before cutting it and distributing to everyone.

Interrupting Demetrio's daydream, Mr. Morrison asked, "Demetrio, do you play chess?"

"Yes, I do, but not that well. I learned from a friend when I was in the army. I became so 'good' at it, Mr. Morrison, that I never beat him."

"Now that we know each other better, Demetrio, please call me Robert. When we are through with dinner, let's play a few games of chess. What do you say? I'll try to teach you a few tricks of the game."

Demetrio smiled. "If you teach me the kind of tricks that the cat taught the tiger, then I'll never beat you either."

Robert looked puzzled.

"My father used to tell me a parable about the cat and the tiger," Demetrio explained. "One day the cat and the tiger met each other and decided to become friends. ' My little cat, I love you,' the tiger told the cat. 'You know, we come from the same family.' 'I love you too, Tiger,' said the cat, and rubbed against the Tiger's mighty paws. 'I see how you love and protect me.' The cat and tiger played together day after day, and the cat taught the tiger her tricks.

'One day, the tiger climbed a tree and stretched out on a giant limb. The cat stretched out directly below, taking advantage of the shade. The tiger looked down at the cat, suddenly feeling hungry. She extended her large tongue, licked her chops, and pounced. But the wily cat sprung into a backflip and catapulted herself out of harms way. The Tiger looked surprised and hurt. 'You never taught me that trick,' Tiger said to the cat accusingly. 'If I had taught you all my tricks,' the cat replied, 'you would have eaten me by now.'"

Robert laughed heartily. "That's a great parable, Demetrio. But I promise you that I will be more forthcoming with my secrets than the cat."

By now they had finished dinner and were drinking coffee. "Do you know, Demetrio, that at the bank we have a lot of Greek customers? Here at Salt Lake City there is a large Greek community. Cathy, you should take Demetrio see the Greek Church."

"Dad, I didn't even know there was a Greek Church here in town."

"Sure there is. I went to a wedding there about a year ago. Nicholas, a Greek friend of mine, had a friend whose son was getting married and he invited me to attend. The ceremony was beautiful, and when it was over the couple walked out of the church followed by their friends and relatives. People kept throwing handfuls of rice, sugarplums and rose petals over them, calling out best wishes. My friend handed me a handful of rice and told me to throw it at the couple because it would bring fertility. Then we all went to a Greek restaurant where there was music and dancing. The party lasted till the early morning hours. Your countrymen are party lovers, Demetrio. They are also good people and know how to have fun.

Nick told me that Greek immigrants started coming to Utah at the turn of the century. Most worked in the coal-mines or on the railroads. They built a church in 1905, on the site where the present church stands today. Now that we are done with religious matters, Demetrio, let's go play a round of chess," he said.

Cathy and her mother sat on the couch talking, as the two men became engrossed in their game. A little after 11:00, the women retired to bed. Hours later, Robert glanced at his watch.

"My god! It's 1:00 o'clock, Demetrio!" he exclaimed. "Let's go to bed, and we can continue the game tomorrow." Then he laughed. "Maybe the day after tomorrow, since tomorrow we're going bowling. Good night, Demetrio."

"Good night, Robert, and thank you for the chess lessons. From what I can see you could probably compete with Kasparov. I hope, before I leave, to win at least one game."

Demetrio went straight to his room. He opened the door, turned on the light and started taking off his clothes. Only then did he realize that Cathy was sleeping under the covers in his bed. Demetrio turned off the lights and slipped in next to her trying not to make any noise. He had not settled down yet when Cathy suddenly jumped out from under the sheets. "Did you think I was sleeping?" she asked falling in his arms and hugging him tightly.

Cathy loosened her arms a bit and looked up at Demetrio "I can't even count the hours I've been waiting for you!" she said with a smile. "You sure took a long time with that game. When my Dad finds somebody to play chess with, he doesn't want to let go. Tell me now, did you win any games?"

"What kind of a question is this, Cathy? Of course not. Your father is unbeatable."

"Well, I don't know of anyone who has beat en him yet," she admitted. Then she kissed him. "Shall I sleep with you tonight?"

"Koukla, I'd love that very much."

"I just have to remember to go back to my room before dawn. Every morning before leaving for work, my Dad quietly opens my door, sticks his head in and whispers to me to have a nice day and that he'll see me later. It doesn't matter if I'm awake or asleep. He started doing this when I was a little girl, and he still does it whenever I'm home."

CHAPTER 18

What a nice sleep I had, Cathy said to herself, when she woke up that Friday morning. Then she stared at the ceiling for a while. Her thoughts traveled back to the past. She remembered how peaceful her life had been several years before. She had fun bowling, going to the lake, hiking in the parks, and just being with the people she loved. She couldn't believe that she had had the courage to leave home for a joyless life in Los Angeles, where she worked in an unsatisfying job during the day, and spent the nights in clubs among strangers, hoping to find someone for companionship.

Cathy slowly got up from bed and went to stand in front of the window overlooking the garden. She pulled back the drapes and sunlight came flooding in warming her face. Then she saw Demetrio in the backyard feeding the birds that were flying around him. She knocked at the glass with her finger hoping that he would hear her. Then she opened the window and yelled out joyously.

"Good morning, Demetrio," she called.

"Good morning, Koukla. Today is a really nice day."

"Have you had breakfast, Demetrio?"

"Not yet. Your mother is in the kitchen. I think she is preparing something. Come down so we can have breakfast together."

"First I'll take a quick shower," Cathy replied, quickly drawing back from the window.

By the time Cathy ran downstairs, Demetrio was already sitting at the kitchen table talking with Cathy's mother.

"Good morning, mom."

"Good morning, Demetrio," she said, sitting next to her mother. They sat together for a few moments talking over the day's plans, and then Demetrio and Cathy went outside and sat on the swing that hung suspended between the branches of two towering oak trees.

"Koukla, can you tell me something?" asked Demetrio softly as though he didn't want anyone else to hear. Cathy looked at him for a moment.

"What is it you want me to tell you?"

"Does your mother have any idea That weare sleeping together?"

"Yes, she knows," Cathy answered immediately.

"She knows? How did she find out?"

"I told her. My mother and I are very close, and I can't hide any secrets from her."

Demetrio suddenly looked troubled.

"What's the matter Demetrio? My mother knows very well that I am not a little child any longer. Do you think she would believe me if I told her we were just friends?"

"No, no. I didn't mean it that way. I just don't feel comfortable. Tell me, does your father know?"

"I don't know. I never asked my mother about it. I am almost sure he does, though. Besides, I don't think it's such a big secret. Do you? Come on, now," Cathy said embracing him. "It's no big deal."

Later that morning, Cathy and Demetrio went back to Temple Square and visited Abravanel Hall, home of the Utah Symphony Orchestra. The Hall glittered with 12,000 square feet of 24-carat gold leaves, a mile-long brass railing, and majestic crystal chandeliers. The hall had taken three years and $12 million to build. It was a gem of a building, and Demetrio was impressed.

On their way out, they stopped in front of a magnificent fountain that graced the front courtyard. "You should see how beautiful it looks on the days the symphony plays," Cathy said.

"Why does it look better then than it does today?" asked Demetrio.

"Because, Demetrio, on concert nights they turn on the fountain's many colored lights – it is quite lovely," she explained.

"Yes, my sweet teacher!" Demetrio replied with a smile.

Then Cathy asked, "Now, where should we go?"

"Koukla, I prefer we go back home. But it's up to you. What do you want?"

"I agree with you," replied Cathy. "That way we can be with my mother and keep her company for a while. She has been by herself in the house most of her life."

They returned home, and Cathy put on an apron and went in the kitchen to help her mother. Her father came home a short while later, carrying two large vases brimming with red and white roses. When Cathy saw him, she ran up to him and threw her arms around his neck. "Daddy, are these for me?"

Cathy's father handed the flowers to her, and gave her a hug and kiss. "Happy birthday, sweetheart," he said. "We are very happy that you are with us once again."

That same evening, Demetrio was introduced to bowling. The bowling alley had 18 lanes, and the sound of balls rolling down the wooden lanes and smashing into pins echoed loudly. Demetrio and Cathy sat at a table directly behind the two alleys where Cathy's father's team was playing and tracked his progress by the giant electronic scoreboard.

"Cathy, how long does the game last?"

"They play three games, each lasting about an hour. So it'll take about four hours or so. Demetrio, I have an idea. Why don't we try our luck and bowl a few?"

"Koukla, I don't even know how to hold the ball."

Cathy took him by the hand. "Let's get out of the way and go to a corner lane. I'll show you how it works." They paid their fee, rented bowling shoes, and found an empty lane at the corner of the alley. Cathy was a practiced bowler, easily knocking down most of the pins. Demetrio, on the other hand, had trouble keeping the ball out of the gutters. Cathy laughed at his clumsiness, and tried to show him how to step into the lane and how to hold and release the ball. After a while Cathy asked how Demetrio was enjoying the sport.

" It's fun – even though I need a lot of practice!" he replied. "Let's come back and do this again before we leave town."

They went over to see how her father's game was going. "When Dad's team is losing, he mopes as if the World Cup were at stake," Cathy explained. Fortunately, his team won three-to-one, and Robert was jubilant. On the drive home, he bragged happily about his team's exploits, as well as his own. "In the last game, Cathy, I scored 242 points with six consecutive strikes. My average today was 216 pins. This season, I am sure we'll win the championship. Last year we lost it in the very last game."

"I'm sure you'll win this year, Dad," Cathy replied. "You know, Demetrio and I bowled a few games tonight."

Robert turned his head a little to glance at Demetrio who was seated in the back seat. "Did you like bowling, Demetrio?"

"I don't think it's an easy game, even though it sometimes looks that way."

Robert laughed. "That's for sure. To get good, you really have to practice almost every day for a few years."

When they arrived home, they sat down to a late dinner and talked of Cathy's birthday party. "I've invited quite a few people," Robert said. "Including Nicholas, who's coming with his wife and daughter."

"Who's Nicholas?" Demetrio asked.

"The Greek guy I spoke to you about, the one who invited me to the Greek wedding in the Orthodox Church."

"Oh, yes. Now I remember," Demetrio said.

"Dad, I've also invited some of my friends from school," Cathy said. "And Michael promised to come and bring his banjo."

Cathy's mother gave her daughter a stern look. She quickly changed the subject. After dinner, Cathy offered to make coffee for them.

"Thank you, sweetheart," her father said. " But I have to say good night and go to bed because I am a little tired tonight. Cathy's mother got up. "I don't want coffee either, Cathy. You two stay up and have your coffee. Goodnight, and we'll see you tomorrow."

When they were alone, Cathy went up to Demetrio and sat on his lap. "We had a beautiful day today, don't you think, my darling?"

"Koukla, when I am with you, everything looks fine to me."

Cathy wrapped her arms around his neck. "Would you like it if I came later to sleep with you, or are you tired of me?"

Demetrio hugged her firmly. "Koukla, these kind of thoughts should never cross your mind."

Later, they lay in each other's arms and talked again about her birthday. "Are a lot of your school friends coming?" Demetrio asked.

"About 24 of them," Cathy answered.

"But Michael is coming for sure," Demetrio said.

Surprised, Cathy turned to look at him. "Why do you ask about Michael?"

"I was just wondering because your mother was uncomfortable when you mentioned his name at dinner tonight."

Cathy snuggled deeper into his arms. "Do I detect some jealousy?" she asked.

He smiled nervously. "No, Koukla. I have no right to be jealous. However, as you know, we men are egotists, and by no means willing to compromise and share with someone else the favors of a woman we love."

Cathy did not answer. "Are you crying again, Koukla?" he asked. "Why are you crying?" He leaned to kiss her, and tasted the salt of her tears.

"Michael and I were friends, and we had a little fling. It wasn't anything serious. And you can be sure, Demetrio, from the moment I met you I haven't even thought of another man. I've never loved anyone the way I love you, without any reservations and with such spontaneity. I love you, Demetrio, and I want so much to be with you always."

"Yes, I believe you, Koukla, I believe you."

"As long as we are together, Demetrio, I want you to love me with all your might. I know that the time we have together is fleeting, that soon everything will come to an end and I'll find myself suddenly robbed of you, and lonely. But I promise you I'll be strong and that in the end, I will be all right."

Cathy moved her body closer to Demetrio's. "I am chilly, Demetrio. Hold me tight in your arms, my darling," she whispered.

Demetrio, now silent, tried to control his own tears. He held Cathy until she fell asleep peacefully in his arms. Then he pulled slowly away, covered her with the sheet, and let his thoughts drift freely. He closed his eyes and pictured himself as a child, care free, playing with other children in the village. How did the years pass so fast? How did things go so wrong? His thoughts drifted to Vanda, and he could see her holding their son in her arms. She looked at him with a sad smile. "Cruel life," Demetrio whispered, choking on his frustration and despair. His thoughts tortured him for a while longer before he was able to quiet his mind and fall asleep.

CHAPTER 19

When Demetrio woke up in the morning, he poured two handfuls of cold water on his face and then went to the kitchen. There he found Cathy and her mother—wearing their aprons and with their shirtsleeves rolled up—deeply involved in the party preparations. "Good morning, ladies," Demetrio said smiling.

Cathy ran up to him. "Good morning, Demetrio. Come see what we've done."

Cathy and her mother had set tables up throughout the garden, covered in bright yellow tablecloths. Colorful bouquets of balloons decorated the garden and graced the entryway to the house. The roses that Robert had brought were set on the long buffet table, that would soon be filled with inviting dishes.

"This is beautiful, Koukla," Demetrio said.

They worked a while longer before changing clothes for the Tabernacle.

Everything that morning was beautiful. Many people had turned out for the Saturday services, and Demetrio saw old people, young families, and teenagers all dressed up. They joined together in worship as the choir sang and the organ resonated joyfully throughout the Tabernacle. Demetrio dreamed he was in heaven. After the service, they headed home. A few of Cathy's friends had arrived to help with the preparations. Demetrio helped Robert unload cases of refreshments from the car and put them in ice-filled coolers. "Robert, I would like to buy a present for Cathy," Demetrio said as they were putting the last of the refreshments on ice.

"Let's go together," Robert said. "At least for now, our job here is finished." As they got in the car, Robert asked Demetrio what he was thinking of buying for Cathy.

"To tell you the truth, I have no idea yet. What do you think is appropriate?" Demetrio replied.

"Hmm... Cathy is a very simple person. She doesn't like jewelry. You probably noticed that the only ring she wears is the one I gave her, with the zephyr stone. I know what!" he suddenly exclaimed with a big smile. "There's a store on Main Street that has everything under the sun. Let's just go there and see what strikes us."

They entered the store a little later, and Robert led Demetrio to the gift section. Demetrio saw a display of all kinds of dolls. He thought of Cathy in her backyard, petting the deer, feeding the geese and the chickens, and gathering eggs in her basket. He thought how she hadn't seemed to have lost any of the happiness or exuberance of childhood. "I've got it," he said, turning to Robert. "I'm going to buy her a doll."

"Whatever you like, Demetrio," said Robert smiling.

Demetrio looked carefully at the selection. Finally, he chose a small Native American princess with long black braids, a dress with colorful beads and a bright band tied around her forehead. The salesman, a dark complexioned man with a broad face, long black hair tied in a pony tail, and a friendly smile said, "Sir, you made a good choice. You can be sure that your little girl will be pleased."

Demetrio looked at the man closely. "What's your nationality?" he asked.

The man straightened up to his full height. "I'm Sioux," he replied with great pride.

Cathy had told Demetrio that Native American tribes had lived in Utah for more than 15,000 years before they were decimated by white settlers and expelled from their ancestral lands. The survivors were forced onto horrible government reservations. These proud people who lived free as the birds ended up enslaved by the inhuman, murderous greed of white people.

"Demetrio, I see you are sad," Robert said as they walked out of the store. "What's bothering you?"

"Nothing, Robert. It's just that this doll and the salesman made me think of the Native Americans and the injustice that they live with everyday."

"You shouldn't be so sensitive, Demetrio. Since man stepped on this earth, there have been injustices. There is no beginning and no end to them."

"Yes, Robert. You are right. You are absolutely right. We live in a crazy, crazy world."

Cathy's guests began arriving later that afternoon, dressed in jeans, plaid shirts, and cowboy hats, western skirts and leather boots, wide leather belts with shiny buckles. They filled the living room and garden with their chatter and laughter.

Demetrio moved away from the friendly strangers and retrieved the doll from Robert's car. Then he slipped quietly and unobserved into Cathy's room. He lay the doll on Cathy's pillow with a note that read, 'Just a little koukla for my Koukla.'

As he was coming down the stairs, he heard Robert calling to him. "Demetrio, come here. I want to introduce you to Nicholas. He is the friend I talked to you about."

Demetrio approached Robert's group. "Nice to meet you, Nicholas," he said, shaking his hand.

"I am pleased to meet a newly arrived fellow countryman. This is my wife, Olga," said Nicholas.

"What brings you to Salt Lake City?" asked the woman standing next to Nicholas, extending her hand in greeting.

"I am just passing through," replied Demetrio somewhat awkwardly.

"Somewhere around here is my daughter," said Nicholas, looking around the room. "Oh, there she is. Dina..." He called out, lifting his hand to get her attention. The young woman approached. "Sweetheart, I'd like you to meet Demetrio who came to town just a few days ago."

"Pleased to meet you," Dina said. She was an attractive young woman, with a sweet smile, not more than 18 years old.

Demetrio returned the greetings politely and thought how beautiful she was. From one end of the room, a band began to play and some of the guests had already started to dance.

"Demetrio, let's go out in the garden so we can talk," suggested Nicholas as he put his hand on Demetrio's shoulder in a friendly gesture. "Where are you from, Demetrio?" asked Nicholas when they were outside.

"I am from Ipiros. How about you, Nicholas?"

"I am a Cretan, from Iraklio. I came to America in 1950, as soon as I got through with my army service. My older brother sponsored me. When I first came, I lived with him in New York, out in Long Island. My brother still lives there with his family."

"Tell me, Nicholas, how did you get here to Utah?"

"In 1964 I came here on a tour with a group of Greek friends I knew from work. I liked the area very much. Since I couldn't stand the winter and cold of New York, I thought this was the perfect opportunity to get out of there. How about you, Demetrio, when did you come to America?"

"I came a few years ago to Los Angeles to visit my uncle and stayed there."

"What kind of work you do, Demetrio?"

"I do maintenance work on my uncle's apartments."

"How many apartments are we talking about?"

"Oh, around 70."

"Seventy? In other words, your uncle is rich!"

"I wouldn't call him a millionaire."

Cathy came up to Demetrio and Nicholas. "Here you are, Demetrio. I've been looking all over for you," she said grabbing his arm. "Let's dance now. I hope you don't mind if I take Demetrio from you," Cathy said to Nicholas with a smile.

After a few dances, Demetrio left Cathy in the company of her friends and went back to Robert and Nicholas. But he kept an eye on Cathy. He wondered who this Michael person was.

Demetrio noticed that Cathy kept dancing with a handsome blond man who seemed to have a lot to say to her — when he wasn't playing a banjo in the band. Demetrio felt his stomach tightening up. "What's happening to me?" he wondered. "Am I going to be battling jealousy now?"

By now Olga had joined their group. Demetrio realized that she was much younger than her husband and very attractive. They moved toward the garden where the sound of the music was less intense so they could hear each other better.

"Demetrio, I noticed you dance very well," said Olga.

Demetrio smiled. "I only know a few steps that Cathy taught me. I have to practice a lot more to improve."

"Would you like to dance with me?" Olga asked.

Demetrio looked at Nicholas. "You have my permission," Nicholas said. "I have not danced for years now. If it's not my arthritis, it's my rheumatism torturing me." Then laughing, he put his hand on Robert's shoulder. "It's old age, dear friend. What a curse."

Olga took Demetrio by the hand and led him back towards the house. As they danced, Olga pressed her body close against Demetrio's. She looked up at him and asked, "Demetrio, is Cathy your girlfriend?"

Demetrio did not respond.

"Would you like to get me a drink?" she asked.

"In this house, they only have soft drinks and water," said Demetrio.

"Then let's go somewhere else," she said winking.

"Olga, how can we do this? Nicholas is here."

"Hm... I don't give a damn if he is here or not. He is no longer the man for me."

"Olga, why are you saying this?"

"For years now, he's been out of commission."

"What do you mean, out of commission?"

"It means that his birdie no longer sings. Not that it was ever that good. He always had a hard time with the high notes. Now, the poor bird can't even make a chirp."

Demetrio broke out laughing.

"Now let's go out for some fresh air," Olga said. "I want to talk to you."

"Out? Where?" Demetrio asked.

"Let's go to my car. There we can sit and talk."

Olga's car, a late model Mercedes, was parked up the street from Cathy's house. As soon as they were inside, Olga took Demetrio's hands in hers, leaned over, and kissed him on his lips.

"What are you doing?" asked Demetrio, opening the car door.

"Okay, okay. Let's just talk. I promise you, I am not going to attack you. Please, at least hear me out."

Demetrio nodded.

"I made the mistake of marrying a man who was my grandfather's age."

Demetrio looked surprised. "But why did you marry him? Did your parents force you to do it?"

"No, no. I cannot say that anyone put pressure on me. I wanted to get married. I was a young and immature village girl. When I heard about going to America, I thought I was very fortunate. All kinds of doors would open to me and my life would be easy and comfortable. My problem started from the day I married Nicholas. He struggled for weeks in bed before he succeeded. I had no experience and I thought that was normal lovemaking. I was very sorry for him for having to work so hard. Sweat was running down his wrinkled body like a river, and I was trying to dry him up with a towel. When reality hit me, it was too late. I was far from my home, relatives and friends, and with my belly full out to there."

"Tell me, Olga, how did you meet Nicholas?"

Olga gripped his hands. "It certainly was not love at first sight. Nicholas had come to Iraklio one summer for vacation and was looking for a wife. The word spread around and pretty soon it was known throughout the villages. My mother happened to have a relative who was Nicholas's neighbor. Then things started happening at the speed of light. I decided to marry him even before I met him— if he wanted me, of course. Do you know why?"

Demetrio shook his head.

"Because I had heard the terrible things that had happened to him. Three years before he came to my village he had lost his wife and 16-year-old twin daughters in an airplane accident. When I found out, I felt so sorry, I wanted to marry him and help him overcome the difficulties he was going through. Yes... I can't deny it; I also wanted to see America! Think of it Demetrio, I didn't even know how old he was. When he came to my home to meet me accompanied by the matchmaker, I was shocked. What I saw was a chubby man with a nice striped, light blue suit, shiny brown leather shoes, a pink shirt with a multicolored tie, and thick prescription glasses.

"Up to that time, I had never been kissed. At night in bed I would squeeze a pillow between my legs as I fantasized about a handsome fairy tale prince. But the man that appeared before me was nothing like the prince of my dreams. He was an old, puffy man with rounded cheeks, with his thin gray hair barely covering the back of his head, and with an overdeveloped belly. The only attractive thing about him was the flowers he was holding awkwardly in his hands.

"Shortly after we met, we had a quick wedding and a little later, 'from the cold winter roots, a lily sprouted up,' as a beautiful Greek song says. The 'winter roots' were the cold nights which I was required to spend in Nick's flabby bosom, and the 'lily' is my daughter Dina. Do you like my life story, Demetrio? Have you ever heard such a love story before?"

Demetrio took her hand. "I am very sorry, Olga. I am truly sorry."

"Don't feel sorry before you hear the whole story. For the past few years, Nick has been impotent. He tells me that his dick is only good for pissing. But Demetrio, I am young and still full of desire."

"Olga, please stop. I don't want to hear anymore of this."

"You promised you'd listen. I'm telling you exactly what is going on. Now I am going tell something else. The drawer of my dresser is full of dildos."

"Olga, what do you mean?"

"I gratify myself by myself."

"What? And Nicholas?"

"My dear husband sits on the edge of the bed and watches me like an idiot. Every time I come, he looks with his eyes wide open and begs me not to stop, hoping that his birdie might finally wake up."

"And after that?"

"There is no 'after,' Demetrio. When I see him naked with his fat belly sticking out, I get turned off. Now I don't even let him watch me. If he wants to watch the show, it has to be live show. Do you get what I mean?"

"No."

"I'll do it with another man and let him watch."

"What you are telling me, Olga, is abnormal."

"It is not as abnormal as you think. A friend of mine does it, and her husband is happy with the arrangement. She even takes vacations with her lover. Demetrio, I want you to understand I am looking to find what I am missing. What is a hungry person trying to find?"

"Food."

"Good. I am glad you caught on. Now, tell me, are you staying in town for a while?"

"I don't know yet. I think sometime next week we are leaving."

"If I give you my phone number, do you promise to call me before you leave? You must come to my house so I can offer you some coffee. It would be terrible if we let a fellow countryman go without showing some of our hospitality."

Demetrio looked at her puzzled. "But what about your daughter, your husband? What are they going to say about it if they see me in your home?"

"Dina goes away to college in the morning and returns in late afternoon. My old man, all he thinks about is how to make another real estate deal. For years now he has been slaving away for the almighty dollar, as though we don't have enough to eat. The income he brings in is enough to feed 10 large families. But Nicholas is a workaholic. He is not interested in anything else. And he has been like this from the time we were married. It was my bad luck to marry this man," whispered Olga, with disappointment and anger.

"Olga, why don't you get a divorce?"

"I'd like that very much, but Nicholas begs me to stay with him."

"Yeah. I understand. Perhaps he wants to avoid the social stigma of a divorce."

"Nick doesn't really care about that."

"Then, what's the problem?"

"He doesn't want to lose half of his wealth. That's why he is willing to do anything for me."

"It's a very difficult situation," Demetrio said.

"Do you often go back home to Greece, Demetrio?"

"When my parents were alive, I use to go often. Now the only relative I have there is my sister who, fortunately, is married and has her own family."

"Tell me, Demetrio. Are you married?"

"Olga, can we change the subject? Tell me, how often do you go to Greece?"

"Every summer. I go to Greece by myself and stay there as long as I want. I can take you there with me if you would like."

"Olga, are you joking? You are a married woman. How can you take me with you?"

"Demetrio, didn't I tell you? My husband is just interested in making business and does not care about anything else."

"What about your daughter?"

"Dina has come with me a few times, but she prefers to spend her vacation here with her own friends."

"From what I understand, you have a lot of fun when you go to Greece."

"More than that. I get plenty of sun and plenty of sex."

"I can understand about the sun. I don't get how you get the sex part."

"It's very simple. I rent a car with a driver."

"So what?"

"You can imagine the rest. I don't have to go into the details."

"Olga, I think you are trying to drive me nuts."

"Now, Demetrio, I will tell you about one of my interesting adventures. One year, my driver was a Turk."

"A Turk? And you took a Turk?"

"Sure I did."

"You are telling me you would go with a Black man?"

Olga laughed. "Why not? I am not a racist. It's been proven statistically that Black men are better lovers than whites. Unfortunately, there were no black drivers in Iraklio. Now, let's get back to the Turk, Kazim. That was his name. He was the sweetest and most energetic driver I ever met. First, he drove me crazy with massages. I mean full massages."

"You mean, you lived together?"

"Sure, he was my driver day and night. During the day, he drove me around to see the tourist sights, and at night he drove me to pleasure palaces. Unfortunately, I went back last year and found out that an American tourist had fallen in love with him and had taken him back with her to Miami. She was a lucky woman, also a smart one. I was stupid not to have done that myself."

"Olga, what you are telling me is hard to believe."

"Perhaps, but these stories are true. Now, Demetrio, that I have confessed everything to you, will you be kind to me?" Olga said, kissing him and pulling him closer. She started unbuttoning his shirt and kept kissing lower, and lower. Demetrio offered no resistance.

"Olga, I can't stand this anymore," Demetrio tried to say as she blocked his mouth with her kisses.

"Let's go to the back seat, Demetrio. It's more comfortable there."

After a few moments, Olga was moaning with pleasure

under Demetrio's body. Then, Demetrio pulled away from her, and started to put his clothes back on. He had lost track of time. The idea that Cathy might be looking for him crossed his mind and he panicked.

"Demetrio, call me before you leave," said Olga as she slipped her hand in his pant pocket.

Demetrio was thunderstruck when he saw that she had left him with a bundle of hundred dollar bills. He looked at her sadly. "I feel sorry for you, Olga. You are really in a sad situation. I am not a gigolo. I am just another man who couldn't resist temptation. Now I am remorseful for what I did." He threw the bundle of bills back at her angrily and opened the car door.

Olga grabbed his hand. "I am sorry, Demetrio. Don't think badly of me. I really want to see you again. Please call me before you go."

Demetrio quickly walked away towards the house. As soon as he got in, he took a soft drink and went to the remotest and darkest corner of the garden where he grabbed a chair to sit. "You pig, you are a dirty, senseless pig," he kept telling himself. "How could you do this? Now, how are we going to face Cathy, you dirty pig?"

"Here you are, Demetrio," he heard Cathy come up beside him. "Why are you sitting here by yourself? I've been looking all over for you. I even looked in your room. Is something wrong, darling?"

Demetrio did not answer. He just squeezed her hands.

"What happened, Demetrio? Are you thinking about the past again?"

"Yes, that's exactly right, memories from the past."

"You forgot me? I am always with you."

"Thank you, Cathy. I am not sure I deserve you."

"Don't say that, Demetrio. Let's go inside. My father and Nicholas have been looking for you."

"Where were you, Demetrio?" asked Nicholas when he saw him.

"I went out in the garden to get away from the commotion."

"By yourself?"

"Yes, Nicholas, because I wanted to talk to myself."

"Don't take life that seriously, Demetrio. I see you are a sensitive person, and that doesn't help in having a happy life."

"How did you get the idea I am a sensitive person?"

"Because I see you always brooding and sad."

"You are right, Nicholas, life is strange. When somebody is happy, then something happens that ruins it all. How about you, Nicholas, are you happy with your life?"

"I cannot say I am happy. As far as that is concerned, who knows what happiness really is? For a while, my life was beautiful. I had a wife who loved me, and two precious daughters who adored me. I loved them more than anything in the world did. If we measure happiness by those standards, then I can say I was extremely happy. Suddenly, they were lost. They were traveling to Greece to visit my sick mother-in-law and the plane crashed. Since then, I don't believe in anything, neither happiness nor unhappiness. I try to live my life without being a burden on other people." He put his hand on Demetrio's shoulder. "Did you notice Olga, how she is still young and beautiful?"

"Sure I noticed."

"Well, she doesn't care about me as a man at all. It's not only that she doesn't love me – she hates me."

"Don't say that, Nicholas. Why would she hate you?"

"She blames me for her unfulfilled dreams. I'm older and sex is a thing of the past for me. But she is young and her blood is boiling. It's natural for her to want romance and physical love. Don't you think?"

"I don't know, Nick. These things are too complicated for

me. How can one find a solution to such a difficult problem?"

"I found the solution."

"What do you mean?"

"I allow her to live the life she likes. That way Dina has a mother, and at home I have a woman to do the house chores. I have no doubt that Olga cheats on me."

"What? How do you know that?"

"One time, Demetrio, she came back from Greece pregnant and she had an abortion."

"Nicholas, I can't understand how you tolerate this behavior."

"It's worse than just cheating," Nicholas confessed. "Some nights Olga brings another man into our bed. In the beginning, I was horrified. Then, I began to accept it."

"That's unbelievable. That's going too far. You shouldn't stand for that."

"I don't think I can stop her. I wish I had your youth, your body and looks. The only thing remaining in me is the desire to do it. Before you leave town, Demetrio, you must come visit us. I invite you for dinner. I am sure tha my wife will be pleased."

Just then, Olga joined them. "Here you are. What are you discussing?"

"We were talking about you," Nicholas said.

"About me? Tell me what you were saying about me."

"I invited Demetrio to come over to the house one evening to have dinner with us. I hope you don't object."

"Not only do I not object – I insist that he does," she said laughing. "You will come, Demetrio, won't you?"

"I am not sure, I have to ask Cathy."

"Why do you have to ask Cathy?" Nicholas asked. "Is she your wife?"

"No, she is not my wife. Simply because I am her guest."

"Let's go over and ask Cathy right now," said Olga.

"No, not right now. I will talk to her later and I'll call you," Demetrio said.

Nicholas pulled out a business card and handed it to him. "You can call me at the office till 5:00 p.m. After that, you can find me at home. Olga is home all day."

"Thank you for the invitation. I'll call you."

"Do you promise?" Olga asked.

"Yes, I promise."

"Now let's go have a soft drink together."

Nicholas saw them walk away together, arm-in-arm, and felt a momentary pang of jealousy. Then he felt nothing.

As Demetrio was walking off with Olga, Michael was dancing with Cathy.

"Michael, let's go out to the garden for a little while. I want to rest a bit," Cathy said, and Michael followed her out.

When they were seated on a low wall at the edge of the pond, Michael turned to Cathy and said, "I never believed I would see you again. Since you left, I haven't found anyone I've cared for as much. Even though there was nothing ever serious between us..."

"We did have fun, though," Cathy replied.

"Tell me something, Cathy. Your mother spoke to me about Demetrio and told me he is a friend of yours. Seriously, Cathy, how close are you to him?"

"Michael, don't ask me details on this one. If you feel something for me, then wait for me because soon I am coming back. First, I have to take care of some business in Los Angeles. When we see each other again, I am going to tell you more about it, okay?"

"Okay," agreed Michael and gave her a quick kiss.

From the window, Demetrio spotted Michael and Cathy in the garden and, as he watched them, he began to feel that they were destined to spend their lives together.

CHAPTER 20

The night wore on, and Demetrio finally slipped off to bed. He waited for Cathy, convinced that she was still with Michael, and felt the sharp sting of jealousy in his heart. After a while, he gave up waiting and fell asleep. He woke up in the middle of the night to a soft caress. In the darkness he saw Cathy holding the doll he had bought her. She bent down and kissed him. "Our little girl wants to tell you goodnight," she said softly.

Demetrio took her hand. "Do you like my little gift? I really didn't know what else to get you."

"Demetrio, this little doll is the most beautiful thing you could have given me. The dining room table is full of gifts. None of those means as much to me as this little Indian girl. Thank you very much, darling. It is the best present I ever received in my whole life. Tonight, Demetrio, I am not going to stay with you because I am very tired. I just came to see you for a little bit. Tomorrow, I will be with you again. Okay?"

Demetrio smiled. "I understand, Koukla. How can you not be tired when you danced all night?"

Cathy kissed him. "Well, goodnight for now. Tomorrow we'll talk again."

"Goodnight, Koukla. And goodnight to you little Indian girl," said Demetrio, shaking her little hand.

The next morning as they were seated at the breakfast table, Robert said to Demetrio, "Nicholas told me he wants to have you for dinner. You should go. You'll get the chance to know each other a little better."

"Yes, Robert, I should go. I'll call Nicholas."

Demetrio thought of Olga and all she could offer him. Then he rebuked himself. "Cathy doesn't deserve this. How would you feel if she did this to you?" hc thought. But another voice prodded him on. Go, don't lose the opportunity," it tempted. "Don't allow life's joys to pass you by. They are offered to you very rarely. Don't you see what happened to Nicholas? Don't feel guilty about Cathy. She is not even married to you. Remember Kazantzakis when he wrote, 'The worst sin for a man is to turn down a woman.'"

That Sunday morning after breakfast, Robert bought tickets for the 5:00 performance at Symphony Hall. At the entrance to the building, Demetrio saw the big fountain and was captivated by the various colored lights mixing with the rising and falling waters. Some children who had escaped their parents' attention were chasing each other around the fountain.

When they came out of Symphony Hall, Demetrio was still truly captivated by the magnificence of the performance. The melodious music was still resonating sweetly through his ears.

Monday morning, Demetrio had made up his mind.

"Cathy, I am thinking of calling Nicholas and going to his house for dinner," he said. "Do you want to come with me?"

"I think the invitation was just for you, Demetrio. As my dad said, it's a good opportunity for you to get to know them a little better."

Demetrio felt relieved. He called Nicholas at his office and arranged for dinner the next night.

When Demetrio arrived at Nick's house he was dumbfounded by the size and opulence of his home. Olga welcomed him, and led him to the living room. She was wearing a low-cut black evening dress and her hair swept up. He and Nicholas talked as Olga brought a bottle of fine cognac and three glasses. Then she excused herself, saying she needed to tend to the hors d'oevres.

"Olga, let the servant do the work and come sit with us," Nicholas said.

"Demetrio is my guest. I want to serve him myself."

"Demetrio, you are a magnet, if I may say so. Olga is crazy about you," Nicholas said smiling as he patted him on the back.

"Nick, to tell you the truth, I don't feel very good about this. I am in your house and I respect that, as I also respect you."

"Come on now, Demetrio, you don't have to feel that way. When it comes down to it, we are still going to be friends. I only wish you could stay here permanently. I could find a good job for you here in town. It's a thousand times better if you are my wife's permanent friend than having all kinds of strange guys around here. With you, I would be less worried about it."

"Nick, I just want to be a family friend. Nothing else."

"Demetrio, please don't play dumb. I thought I made it clear when we were at Cathy's house. If it were not you, for sure it'd be somebody else. I hope this doesn't bother you. As for me, it doesn't bother me, as strange as it might seem. Now I'll tell you something funny. Olga went out and bought white, silk bed sheets. Do you know why? She saved them for you. Tonight, I'll sleep in the guest bedroom."

Olga returned with a large tray full of hors d'oeuvres and sat next to Demetrio.

Demetrio looked at her in amazement.

"Why do you look at me like that? Do you think my husband will become angry? Don't worry, Nick is very nice to me. He never refusesme anything. That's why I love him. Isn't that right, darling?"

Nicholas smiled, looking rather sad.

Later, after dinner was over, Demetrio got up from the table and was ready to leave. Nicholas asked him, "Demetrio, where do you plan to go at this time of night? Sleep here tonight, and tomorrow you can go."

"No, Nicholas, thank you. The Morrisons are expecting me."

Olga cried out, "Nick, darling, call Robert and tell him Demetrio had a few too many drinks and will stay here tonight. Demetrio, come sit on the couch and don't worry about it. Nick will talk to Robert. They are friends, they'll settle it." Then she whispered in his ear, "Didn't we agree you'll sleep with me tonight? Why are you arguing about it?"

"Demetrio, I just talked to Robert. Everything is fine," said Nicholas when he returned to the living room. "Do you know what he told me? ' That you are in good hands.' Now I'll go to my bed. Goodnight," he said, as he walked from the room, his steps heavy.

Demetrio saw that old human mass slowly fade away, and felt truly sorry. "How low can human dignity dip, how low can human humiliation reach?" he asked himself.

"What's on your mind, darling?" Olga interrupted him with a kiss.

"I am thinking about Nicholas. You really humiliated him."

" I don't humiliate him. He is a free person. He can choose what's best for him. For years now I have been trying to do my duty as a faithful wife. However, I have come to the end of the road. I am being honest about it. I don't do it behind his back. Half of the property we have belongs to me, according to the law. I can live like a queen by supporting myself, and selecting the type of lifestyle and friends I want. I don't need Nicholas; he is the one who needs me. Many times I feel sorry for him but what can I do, live in a convent for his sake? Oh, no, I am not going to do that. Life is too short. I want to enjoy it."

"Olga, please, don't get me involved in your problems. I simply expressed my opinion."

"And I want to tell you something else, Demetrio. Nicholas had his chances, like every person. At one time he was also young and had the opportunity to experience happiness and pleasure. Unfortunately, everything has an end. The pleasurable road is over for him and now it's all uphill. That's how life is. It's the same for everyone. Come now, sit close to me and be good to me."

At that moment, Demetrio felt like giving her a hard slap and then running out into the street, but his animal instincts overcame him. He leaned to kiss her, hesitantly. Then he kissed her again while he ran his hands up and down her legs.

"Come, darling, let's go to my room. I have a big surprise for you."

"The white, silk bed sheets?" asked Demetrio.

"How do you know?"

"Nicholas told me."

That night was like a dream for Demetrio. Olga gave him pleasures beyond his wildest dreams. In the morning, when Demetrio opened his eyes, he saw Olga looking at him, smiling as she ran her hands through his dark, rich hair. "Are you awake, my treasure? Sleep some more, if you like. I enjoy you like this; it gives me pleasure to be so close to you."

"What time is it, Olga?"

"Why care about time, darling? Today, stay here with me."

"Olga you squeezed everything out of me all night. What else do you want from me?"

"To fully enjoy you, darling, I have to digest you completely.

What a real man you are! Demetrio, you are worth a lot, but it appears you don't know it. I would give everything I have to have you always with me."

Demetrio laughed. "How much do you give?"

"To have you all to myself?"

"Yes, lets say that, all to yourself."

"I can give you a signed, blank check."

"I am not sure what that means."

"It means about half a million dollars."

"Olga, I'll quote to you a verse from an old Greek folk song, 'Are you making fun of me or are you dead serious?'"

"I am dead serious. To prove it, I promise to make you a full partner in my share of the property."

"How about Nick?"

"Fuck Nick! He doesn't count. Do you agree? And to be rid of him, we can go live in Greece."

"Olga, I think you are crazy. Is this how you squander your wealth, with the first guy you come across? This only happens in Hollywood films."

"Our life, Demetrio, is like a movie. For some, the movie is a comic tragedy, for others a musical, and for still others a big drama."

"Olga, I need to take a bath. I've had enough for today."

"Demetrio, can you come one more time before you leave town?"

"No, Olga. That's impossible."

"Demetrio, I'll make a proposition to you. Only I don't want to hear any silliness about pimping, or being sorry, or other stupidities."

"Let's hear it. What is your proposition?"

"I'll pay you every night you spend with me. Tell me your price."

"In other words, you are offering to buy me?"

"Yes, I want that very much. But since I can't buy you, I'll rent you."

"I am worth 10,000 per night," said Demetrio seriously.

"To show you how generous I am, for the first night I'll double it, and then 10 each after that."

Olga put on her robe and went across to the dresser. She returned with her checkbook in hand. She wrote a check and handed it to him. "Tell me when you are coming again so I can write one for the second visit."

"Olga, you are really crazy. You pay 20,000 for one night's pleasure."

"I only pay that for a good stud. Now listen to me, Demetrio. We have more than $ 30 million dollars in stocks. Our savings account is over $ 5 million. Each month we have seventy thousand net from rents, besides what Nicholas earns from his job, not an insignificant amount. From the rental properties we have in Iraklio, on the beach, I have no idea how much we have accumulated. How can we spend all that, Demetrio? We only have one daughter. I am nearly 40 yars old. I don't drink, gamble, or smoke. I only have one vice – lovemaking. That's my raison d'etre. Well, what do you say now, do you still think I am crazy?"

"I don't know, Olga. Things look confusing. I'll go take a bath now, and if you like, you can join me."

"Yes, I'd like that very much. I think it's very sexy to see your naked body."

Later they went down to the kitchen where Olga prepared a very delightful breakfast for the two of them. "Well, Demetrio, are you taking the check or not?"

"Of course not. I thought I made it clear to you."

"At least allow me to give you a present."

"You can give me a necktie," said Demetrio smiling.

"I'm going to think of something more permanent so you

won't forget me. Demetrio, I'll tell you something else which you should consider very seriously."

"What's that?"

"I'll give you my card with my phone number and address. Keep it in a safe place. It's like an insurance policy for you. If you ever need me, wherever you might be, I'll come to meet you. If you ever come across hard times, always remember that in Salt Lake City you have a faithful and powerful friend who can be of great help in time of need."

"Thank you, Olga. I know that you are a generous friend. I respect that. I only want a small thing from you."

"Whatever your heart desires."

"I don't want Cathy to ever find out about us."

"No, my darling. Nobody else will ever know about this. You have my word. Tell me Demetrio, do you love Cathy?"

" Why do you ask that? Are you jealous?"

"Am I jealous? I am dying from jealousy. But I want you to know I'll never let my jealousy come between you and Cathy. You have an inexhaustible supply of energy for both Cathy and me. Few men can brag about this. I can count them on my fingers."

"Come now, Olga, don't exaggerate. I think you are saying this to flatter me."

"No, I don't exaggerate at all. From what little you know about me, you must have realized I heve plenty of experience with men. Remember when I talked to you about the Turk, Kazim? His only defect was that he got stuck on the uphill."

"What do you mean?"

"After two times, he was done. But you... wild beast, what did your mother feed you when you were young?"

"Acorn nuts!" answered Demetrio laughing. "Before I leave, I'll drop by here to see you one more time Olga, you are a great lover. I enjoy lively women like you."

"Are you telling me the truth? You are not joking, are you?"

"Why would I be joking? I have to find a good excuse to leave the house. Do you know something, Olga? I really like your silk sheets."

"How about me?"

"I like you even more than your sheets."

"Before you go, I want to show you how my idiot husband wastes his money. Do you see this painting?"

"Yes, I see a picture of scattered paints. Don't ask me anything beyond that because I'm completely in the dark about paints."

"Do you know how much these 'paints' cost?"

"I have no idea."

"This painting is a Picasso. Nicholas bid up the price in an auction to $ 180,000."

"What? He paid that much for this trash?"

"Demetrio, paintings by Picasso can sell for up to $ 10 million."

"And who pays this kind of money?"

"Some idiots like my husband who have a lot of money to waste. I also spend, but I enjoy it, I get a lot of pleasure out of it. Nicholas gets his kicks by looking at Picasso's scattered paints. Do you see now why I don't care about money? Now, do you see why I am asking you to help me spend some of it?"

When Demetrio returned to Cathy's house, it was 11:00 a.m. Cathy ran up to him and hugged him. "Tell me, Demetrio, how was your night? Did you sleep well? I missed you, darling. Why didn't you call me to come pick you up?"

"That's okay, Koukla. Olga offered to give me a ride."

"Tell me, did you have a good time?"

"Very good. They really went out of their way to make me comfortable. I couldn't thank them enough. Now they insist on having a special going away dinner for me. I hope it's okay with you, Koukla. They were so generous with me that I didn't have the courage to say no."

"I think you did the right thing. Knowing people like them is always useful. Did you know that Nicholas is one of the richest people in town? My father thinks very highly of him. He always helps out those in need and contributes a lot of money to hospitals and institutions for the poor."

"Cathy, how do you know these things about them?"

"My father told me last night at dinner."

"Koukla, I hope you forgive me for not coming home last night. I drank a little too much and didn't want your parents to see me in that condition."

"You mean, you got drunk?" asked Cathy laughing.

"No, I didn't really get drunk. I just drank more than I should. You see the Greek wines are very tasty and hard to resist."

"Now, Demetrio, do you want to go for a ride downtown?"

"Let's go. If you want to, we can grab something to eat for lunch when we get there."

"That's a good idea, Demetrio. That'll give my mom a chance to rest. She is still tired from the party."

"Why don't we take her along?"

"My mom prefers to stay home."

In a short time they were in the central plaza, walking along the beautifully landscaped trees. "Demetrio, you were away for one night and I felt very strange. I didn't sleep very well because I kept thinking of you. Do you know what I did? I went to your room and slept in your bed. I smelled your sheets and hugged your pillow to feel somehow that I was with you."

"That's what love is all about. Tonight, I'll wait for you, Koukla. I've missed you a lot."

"That's a deal, my beloved prince. Now tell me when you want to leave."

"Whenever you want we go. You are doing the scheduling. If we stayed here for the rest of my life, I'd be the happiest person on earth. Unfortunately, this is impossible."

"My father keeps saying that nothing is impossible for man. Do you think it's not true?"

"I am not sure. Maybe your father is right. Cathy, can you do me a favor?"

"Sure I can."

"Before we leave, can we go to the Greek Church? I want to pray for forgiveness."

"Forgiveness! Forgiveness from who?"

"From God. At some point I had doubted His existence and now I bitterly regret it. Now I realize, whatever happens to a person during his life, it is for the purpose to test his faith."

"Demetrio. Don't worry, God always forgives."

"Cathy, if we get tickets to fly Monday, try to get them for the evening."

"Why at evening?" asked Cathy

"I want to have the opportunity to view the beautiful sunset one more time. It is a sight to behold. The sun disk increases in size as it approaches its setting. Its color tums red like a flame and reflects off the calm surface of the lake. As it descends slowly behind the mountaintops, it splashes an exquisite orange hue across the horizon, which is punctuated with thousands of other colors. As it disappears, I get the impression it is in a slow-motion, dive into the lake."

"That's a very nice description, Demetrio. Our sunsets are very beautiful. Even writers and poets have written about that. The mountains you see there in the far horizon, where the sun disappears as you say, are called Oquirrh Mountains."

"Tell me Koukla, when can I go to Nicholas's house?"

"Are you planning to spend the night there?"

"I'll try not to drink too much retsina."

"I remember retsina from the Acropolis Restaurant in Los Angeles," Cathy said.

"Retsina, Cathy, is the most popular wine of Greece. It quenches the thirst of all Greeks."

"Then you have the right to get drunk on retsina," said Cathy smiling. "It's not going to be the end of the world if you spend one more night at Nicholas's house."

"It's okay with you, Cathy?"

"Even if we were married, I'd still permit you."

"Thank you, Koukla, thank you for your understanding. Well, what day do you think I should go?"

"Friday night I might go bowling with my father."

"Then I'll go Friday." Deep down Demetrio heard the voice of his conscience again telling him, "Liar, hypocrite, pig."

Friday night, when Demetrio went to Olga's house, her daughter Dina was also there. Demetrio noticed that the young lady was looking him over from head to toe. During dinner, he felt her foot rubbing against his leg.

"Olga, your daughter is cute," commented Demetrio late at night as they were lying next to each other in bed.

"How cute?"

"Very cute."

"You Greek devil, what goes through your mind? Do you want to take every woman you come across to bed?"

Demetrio laughed and squeezed her naked body. "Not all of them. Only the cute ones."

"You, Demetrio, possess great magnetism, you rascal. You know what Dina told me? That you are a handsome man."

"Do you believe that too?"

"You are very handsome man, with a capital M. Now that I have gotten to know you better, I will tell you all my secrets. Dina knows we are having an affair."

"Olga, how does she know that?"

"Very simple, I told her. Dina and I don't keep secrets from each other. Dina is a very precocious girl, Demetrio. At thirteen she was asking me questions about sex. You see, in school, besides reading and arithmetic, they learn other things. Dina reads a lot of love stories. She has read *Kama Sutra* many times. She keeps the book next to her bed. I actually think it's the natural thing to do and I am pleased she likes boys. Many of her girl friends play sexual games among themselves because they consider this safe sex."

"I am hearing all this, Olga, and I have a hard time believing it. I must be very naive."

"Tell me, Demetrio, why do you want to go to Brazil? Stay here and you'll never regret it."

"Olga, I can't stay no matter what. I have to go to Brazil."

CHAPTER 21

Demetrio and Cathy spent the next few days keeping Cathy's mother company, and exploring Salt Lake City.

Sunday night, after everyone went to bed, Cathy went to her parents' bedroom and sat next to her mother. "Mom," she said, holding her hands. "I want you to believe me that soon I will be coming back, and this time it will be for good." Then she removed the beautiful gold necklace that her father had given her for her birthday and placed it in her mother's palm, closing her fingers around it. "Keep this, Mother. You can give it back to me when I return." Then she got up and went to her father, who had been silently watching his daughter. Cathy bent down, hugged and kissed him. "Dad, I want to thank you for all you have done for me. I have only given you problems and bitterness."

Her father reached over and stroked her hair. "No, Cathy. What you are saying is not true. We don't say that you gave us only problems and bitterness. People must go through a lot of trials and tribulations. Otherwise they don't understand the meaning of life. When you come back home everything is going to be all right. We will be once again as we were before. You will realize this for yourself. That's why you shouldn't worry. We want to see you always happy. That's what's most important."

Cathy smiled and gave her father a final hug. Then she quietly left, stopping in her room to retrieve the Indian doll before joining Demetrio for the night.

The next morning, Cathy, her mother, and Demetrio were sitting around the kitchen table when Cathy's Dad unexpectedly returned from work.

"Dad!" yelled Cathy when she saw him. "What a nice surprise!"

Her father opened his arms and hugged her. "Since this is your last day at home, my sweet daughter, I thought it would be nice to spend it with you."

"Thank you, Dad. You are always so nice to me."

"Demetrio, how are things?" Robert said as he sat at the table.

"Everything is fine, Robert. The only thing bad is that we are leaving today."

"Demetrio, our house is always open to you and you are always welcome here. You should know that."

"Yes, I must come back, Robert. I want to beat you in a chess game, at least once. You see, it is a matter of honor."

Robert cracked a hearty smile. "I see Demetrio, you are a true Spartan. You hate losing any challenge." Then he turned to Cathy. "What time does your plane leave, sweetheart?"

"At 8:30 tonight, Dad."

"Well, that gives us most of the day. What do you say we all go out for lunch?"

"It's fine with us," replied Demetrio immediately. "Only, you will allow me to treat you today."

As they were getting ready to leave, Nicholas drove up. "Nicholas, what brings you here?" asked Robert.

"I came to say good-bye to my friend. I hope I can have you over again sometime in the future Demetrio," Nicholas said.

Then he pulled a small package from his pocket. "This is a small present for you."

"Thank you, Nick, thank you so much."

"So long for now and have a nice trip. I hope to see you again."

When they arrived at the restaurant, Demetrio opened up the package and found a gold Rolex watch. Robert took it in his hands and looked it over. "That's a very nice present, Demetrio. You know this watch is worth more than $ 10,000."

"Robert, are you sure this watch is worth that much?"

"I am certain, unless it's a fake. I can't imagine it's a fake."

"Robert, I am not used to wearing this kind of a watch. Please keep it and return it to Nicholas."

"No, Demetrio, you cannot do that. It's a big insult to return a present."

They passed the day together very pleasantly. When it was time for Demetrio and Cathy to leave, all four drove to the airport and spent their last minutes together talking in the passenger lounge until the call came for boarding.

"Thank you very much for your hospitality," said Demetrio hugging Cathy's parents good-bye. "I hope some day to treat you as well as you treated me."

"If you want to do that, then you have to promise that you will take good care of our daughter," Robert said.

"I promise you that," said Demetrio solemnly.

Robert turned and hugged his daughter tightly. "We will be expecting you, Cathy," he said. "Try to come back as soon as you can. We can't stand your being away much longer."

Cathy then turned and hugged her mother. "Have a good trip, my little girl," she said with tears rolling down her cheeks. "I pray to God that you return to us soon."

"I will come back, Mom. Please don't cry anymore. I promised you I'll be back very soon."

A few minutes later the plane was lumbering down the runway, and Cathy once again buried her face in Demetrio's shoulder and held on to him tightly. She stayed there until the plane had safely attained cruising altitude, and the engines had quieted and the cabin was no longer shaking.

"Well, Koukla, our vacation is over."

"Yes, Demetrio. But we had a very good time. We planned a one-week vacation and stretched it out more than 40 days." Demetrio kissed her.

"Koukla, I will never forget the good times we've had."

"It's a shame we are not going to ever do this again," said Cathy looking in his eyes.

Demetrio turned his face away and looked out of the window into the dark, empty space.

"Demetrio, I decided to return home as soon as possible. I promised this to my parents. My poor mother has been crying all the time. She still does not believe I will go back."

"Cathy, I am glad you are making the right decision. Knowing that you will be with your parents, I'll feel better, too."

Cathy looked at him sadly. "The time for us to separate is coming so close, so fast," she said. "I can hardly believe that we're not going to be together anymore." She took his hands and held them tightly. "I always thought I was so strong. All the time we've been together I've prepared for this moment, and I was certain that when it came, I would be okay. But now, I'm not sure how I can endure not having you in my life."

A few moments later Cathy was asleep in his arms. Demetrio closed his eyes and tried to fall asleep, too, but his efforts were in vain. In Salt Lake City, his mind had been mostly at ease. But from the moment the plane had taken off for Los Angeles, he felt heavy, disturbed. Unwanted memories from his past plagued him.

When Cathy woke up, she looked at Demetrio.

"I see you are deep in thought again," Cathy said. "What is bothering you?"

Demetrio didn't answer, but pulled her close to his body while the muscles on his face twitched nervously. They did not exchange any more words. They were both absorbed in their own individual thoughts. Cathy imagined Demetrio without responsibilities and without another woman and a child separating them, free to join his life with hers.

The voice of the stewardess interrupted her daydreaming and announced their arrival.

The plane touched down, and the passengers streamed out to claim their baggage. Cathy and Demetrio hailed a taxi and headed to Cathy's apartment. "Back in the jungle," Demetrio muttered as the taxi cruised down Lincoln Boulevard towards Westwood. "If I had not taken our vacation Koukla, I would have thought all of America was like this hellish city."

"I learned something on our trip, too, Demetrio. I learned that I'm done with adventures."

Demetrio looked at her with sympathy. "I wish, Koukla, things were different. I wish, that I didn't have to leave you."

Cathy did not reply. She just leaned her head on his chest. When the taxi reached Pico Boulevard, it turned right and within minutes they stopped in front of Cathy's apartment. "We're home," Cathy said and her eyes brightened with joy. Demetrio paid the taxi driver and, holding his suitcase in one hand and placing the other around Cathy's waist, headed up the stairs. Cathy unlocked the door, dropped her suitcase, and turned to face Demetrio. She stood there, looking up at him.

"Why do you look at me like that, Koukla?" he asked her.

"I am waiting."

"Waiting? Waiting for what?"

Cathy laughed. "I am waiting so you can pick me up and

carry me across our bedroom threshold. I don't know why, but today I feel like a bride."

Demetrio lifted her gently into his arms, touched his lips to hers, and, kicking the door closed behind him, carried her to bed. They did not go out that night.

A little past midnight, Cathy ordered a pizza, and Demetrio offered to go to the store to pick up some beer. As he headed for the door, Cathy called to him.

"Demetrio, didn't you forget something?"

He looked all around, felt his pockets for his keys and wallet, and said, "I don't think so."

Cathy pouted like a child who's been denied a favorite treat.

Demetrio realized his mistake and ran back and kissed her. "That's better," she said smiling. "You should not forget your responsibilities."

"Forgive me, Koukla. I am absent-minded sometimes. That's all." Then he leaned to kiss her again.

In a little while, Demetrio returned with a six-pack. "The pizza is not here yet, Koukla?"

"Any time now," replied Cathy. "It doesn't matter if it takes a little longer. That way we can eat with better appetite. Demetrio, now that we are back in our home, tell me something. What are your plans?"

Demetrio ran his fingers through his hair trying to figure out how to respond. "Cathy, I don't know what to do. I need to call Vanda – it's been six months since the last time I talked with her. I have to talk to Costa, and read the letters from her that he has been keeping for me. It's so difficult. I love you, Cathy. This trip we took together was like a honeymoon for me. I feel in my heart as if you are my wife."

Cathy hugged him. "Come, my darling. Kiss me and don't think of me so much. Consider me as just another love affair."

"Cathy, can you really believe that you are just another love affair? Can't you hear how hard my heart is pounding for you?"

At that moment, the doorbell rang. Demetrio went to get the pizza and brought it to the table. Cathy joined him and they sat together, eating and talking. "Tomorrow, Demetrio, I will call home. I already miss my parents. I can't believe how I've neglected them these past few years – I hardly ever called them, and for a long time they didn't even have my address."

"Come now, Cathy, don't think about this anymore. Just always remember that it's never too late to start again."

The next morning, Demetrio woke up to the delicious smell of coffee brewing. Cathy was sitting at the table.

"Mm..." said Demetrio. "How nice good coffee smells."

"Let me make you some breakfast," said Cathy.

"Wait a little while, Koukla. Let me take a shower first. Did you take a shower yet?" asked Demetrio.

"Oh, yes. I've been up for a while now."

"You didn't wait for me."

Cathy laughed. "I didn't wait for you because I didn't know what time you'd get up. I promise you that tonight we can take a shower together."

Later Demetrio called his uncle to make arrangements so they could meet. "Nephew, now I live in Brentwood. It is a nice and quiet neighborhood. But no matter what I do, Demetrio, I feel very lonely. When we get together we'll talk about it. Where are you now, Demetrio?"

"I am in Westwood."

"You are very close to me. Not even 10 minutes driving distance. Let me give you directions how to come, Nephew. Get paper and pencil and write it down."

"Koukla, would you like to go with me to my uncle's home, or do you have other plans?"

"Demetrio, I don't have any plans. The only thing I have to do is stop by the shop where I worked to say hello to Lena and tell her that I will not be returning to work again. We can go together, we can do it any time. If not today, we can go tomorrow. Then I will stay with you until you take care of your situation. When you leave, Demetrio, I will go back home again. It's the proper time for that."

Demetrio hugged her. "Koukla, maybe we should not have fallen for each other so intensely and bonded our hearts together. You can't imagine how difficult it will be for me to say good-bye to you."

"Come now, Demetrio. We knew from the first time we met that the time would come for us to say good-bye to each other. Let's make the most of the time we have together, and be glad for the love we've known." Cathy remained for a while in Demetrio's arms. It was something like a safe shelter. At these moments at least she felt that Demetrio was completely hers and hers alone.

When they reached Christo's home, Christo came out with open arms. "Demetrio, tell me, where have you been all this time? Where do you live now?" he asked, his eyes damp with tears as he kissed his nephew.

Cathy stood quietly by, watching them with interest. Christo glanced at her and said, "Nephew, who is this woman?"

"Uncle, this is Cathy. Koukla, this is my uncle Christo, the one I've been talking about all the time."

They went inside Christo's house, a two-story building surrounded by windows that let in a flood of light. The back opened to a lovely tree-shaded garden and well-groomed lawn. The three sat down in the living room, and Christo and Demetrio began talking in Greek, remembering the tragedies that had befallen them. After a while, Cathy excused herself. "I am going out into the garden," she said standing up.

"Koukla, forgive us for talking in Greek. We don't have any secrets but we talk in our language because it is easier for us to communicate."

Cathy smiled. "That's okay, darling. I'll be in the backyard."

When Cathy walked away, Christo put his arm on Demetrio's shoulder. "Darling?" he asked. "What does that mean?"

"Uncle, this woman saved my life. I am sure that God felt sorry for me and sent her to me to lighten my burden. Without her, probably I would not be alive now."

"And how about Vanda, who is waiting for you?"

"Cathy knows everything from the very beginning when we met. Even though she loves me, she sacrifices herself and guides me so I can get back with Vanda and my child. She is a wonderful person, Uncle."

"I hope, Demetrio, that God will help you choose the right way." Christo paused. "The day you called to tell me you were okay, I called Eleni. You can't imagine how happy she was, the poor soul. She was crying and laughing at the same time. 'Thank you Virgin Mary,' she kept saying again and again. 'Thank you for being near my brother.' I also called Vanda, but she was not home. I talked with her father and I told him the happy news. Since that day, Vanda has never called again. I also met Costa several times. He has quite a few letters from Vanda for you. As I told you on the phone, Costa has the file that I gave him. In that file you will find all the information about my latest will. I have made you trustee and executor."

"Uncle, please stop talking about wills. I don't feel good about this. You shouldn't have done this."

"Demetrio, I did this because I was afraid my life could come to an end at any moment. Now, Demetrio, I want to tell you something else. Everything is over with my ex-wife. We have come to an agreement that was negotiated by the lawyers. I paid her off and she released all claims against me."

"Tell me, uncle, if your wife had no legal rights on your property, why did you have to pay her off?"

"I wanted to finish this business because the way things were going the lawyers were taking more than the settlement value for the 'missus.'"

"Uncle, I want you to forgive my behavior. When I found out what happened to my family, it was as if lightening hit me. For days and nights I went around like a lost sheep. I found shelter in the dark bars of Sunset Boulevard where I was mostly drunk. In my constantly muddled mind, I was searching for those who caused my misfortune and subconsciously I pointed the finger at you because you insisted we remain in America."

Christo covered his face with his hands and began crying.

"Don't cry, Uncle. I realize my mistake. It's not your fault, not at all." Demetrio went close to his uncle and hugged him. When Christo had calmed down, Demetrio asked, "Uncle, where are Dora and my children resting now?"

"I bought lots in the Santa Monica cemetery. I go there daily with flowers."

"Thank you, Uncle, thank you for everything," said Demetrio and kissed Christo's hands. The two men hugged each other and cried together silentely.

After a while, Demetrio raised the subject of Christo's will again. "Uncle, I appreciate your generosity. But I don't have any rights to your property, and besides, I have to go to Brazil."

"Demetrio, the only thing I ask you to do when you settle down is to send me a letter so I can find you in case I need you, wherever you are. When do you plan to leave?"

"I don't know yet, Uncle. This afternoon I'll try to meet Costa. After I read Vanda's letters, I'll make the final decision."

"In any case, Nephew, please let me know what your decision is. Now, wait a moment."

Christo got up and went upstairs. When he returned he was holding a small envelope in his hand. "This is for you, Nephew."

"What is this, Uncle?"

"Take it and open it when you are by yourself at home. By the way, Demetrio, where do you live now?"

"In Cathy's apartment."

"Don't you want to stay with me until you leave? The house is large. If you stay with me, I won't be by myself, even for a short while."

"Thank you very much, Uncle. I'll ask Cathy and let her decide."

Meanwhile, Demetrio had opened the envelope to find, to his great surprise, a check for $ 10,000. "Uncle, what's this for? So much money for me? I don't need it. At least now I don't have any special need. I can't accept this kind of money. You have my word, if I ever am in need, I will come and ask for help."

"First, listen to me, Demetrio, and try to understand my point, then decide whether you'll take or not. I almost died son. Suddenly I realized we are absolutely nothing. The life of a person is more like a mixed up dream consisting only of a little happiness, many sorrows, and a lot of worries. I came this close, Nephew, to stepping into the nether world. Can you imagine Demetrio? I didn't even have my will. If I had died, my wife and kids would have taken everything and wasted it. They would be making fun of me because not one of them ever thought of me as a human being. Thank God everything turned out okay for me in my life. After all, I have the right to spend everything I made the way I think is right for me. Don't you agree? Go now; call Cathy so we can all have some coffee together. Before you go, let me have your phone number. I want to call you one day so we can go out to have dinner. Okay?"

"Yes, Uncle. We can go over to the Valley. There is a nice Greek restaurant called Acropolis."

"Oh, I know it well," said Christo. "Odysseas, the owner, is my son Nick's godfather. We are very good friends. He will be very happy to see us. The only problem we will have is that he will not let us pay the bill. Odysseas is a very nice and hospitable guy. Go, call the young lady in."

Demetrio called for Cathy, and she came into the kitchen where Christo was making coffee. "Uncle, you and Demetrio sit in the living room. I'll make the coffee," Cathy said with a smile.

"This one is a very pleasant girl," Christo said to Demetrio. " You are very lucky with women, Nephew."

In a little while, Cathy brought the coffee and she sat in a chair opposite the two men. "I have invited you and Demetrio to live with me in this house for as long as you like," Christo said to Cathy. "Demetrio is better than a son to me."

"Uncle Christo, don't ask me about this. Whatever, Demetrio wants, I agree with his decision."

"Demetrio, I have an idea," Christo said. "Why don't we go eat something before you go? Up the street, on Montana Avenue, is an Italian restaurant that has delicious food. When you eat their *pastasciutta*, you want to eat the dish with it."

After lunch, Cathy and Demetrio returned to their apartment, and Demetrio called Costa. They arranged to meet later that evening and Demetrio asked Cathy to accompany him.

"I will stay here, darling," Cathy said. "You go get the letters, and then come right back."

"It will take a while, Koukla, because all of Vanda's letters are in Portuguese. Costa has to translate for me. Come now, Koukla, let's go together. I don't know how to walk by myself anymore. Or, are you getting tired of me?"

Cathy got up at once. "Never," she said, holding him close.

"What do you say now? Are you going to come?" asked

Demetrio smiling. "After that, I promise we'll go out to dinner."

Cathy nodded. "I love you Demetrio. I love you very much."

Costa lived in a rented apartment in Santa Monica. When Demetrio rang the bell, the door opened almost immediately. "Good to see you Demetrio!" said Costa greeting him warmly. "To tell you the truth, I thought you had gone home to Greece."

"No, Costa. I'm still here. How are you doing?"

"Come inside and make yourselves comfortable."

"Costa, this is my girlfriend. Her name is Cathy."

"Hi, Cathy," said Costa shaking her hand.

"I am very pleased to meet you, Costa. Demetrio has told me about you."

"Tell me something Costa, are you here alone?" asked Demetrio.

"Right now, yes. My sister went over to a friend's place."

"How about your son?"

"He is still at school. Today he will be coming late because he has basketball practice. Let me offer you some refreshments and then we can talk."

Costa brought them drinks, and they spent a few moments catching up on old news.

"How is work going Costa?" Demetrio asked.

"Same as always. Construction work is very hard. When I was young and had all kinds of opportunities, I didn't seize them. I believed that life would be always the same. At some point I realized that's not true, but it was too late. My fate was turning the corner, abandoning me with a smile full of irony as though it were telling me 'You will sleep on the bed you've made.' You know what an Egyptian friend of mine told me when I was in Sao Paulo, Demetrio? That those who have been programmed become rich. When I asked him, 'who programs them?' he laughed and answered, 'Don't ask because nobody knows that.' As I see it, Demetrio, I have not been programmed to be rich. Then Costa got up, went into another room and returned carrying a bundle of letters tied up in a string. "In here, Demetrio, in these letters, are all the secrets of your life," said Costa with a smile. Then he untied the string and let the letters fall loose on the table. "Let's see if we can find the beginning and the end in these."

"Let's open them all to look at the dates," suggested Demetrio.

Cathy sat at the table looking at Costa and Demetrio.

"Koukla, unfortunately, here we don't have a garden so you can go for a walk while we are doing this," Demetrio apologized.

"I prefer to be here," Cathy replied. "I am also curious to find out the news."

"Demetrio, first of all I want to tell you something else," said Costa. "A few months ago, maybe back in January if I remember correctly, Vanda sent a letter addressed to me personally asking me if you have being receiving her letters, why you have not shown signs of life, if I knew where you live, and other questions of this sort. Naturally, I answered right away. I told her I didn't know where you were. After that, her letters grew less frequent, and during the last two months I have received only one letter."

Demetrio opened the earliest letter and took out the photographs of his son Costaki that Vanda had sent him. In one photo, Vanda was holding the child in her arms while her parents stood beside her. Cathy took the photographs from Demetrio and examined them closely. "Your son is cute," she said quietly. Demetrio turned and watched as Cathy continued to look at the photos.

Costa picked up the letters and began to translate. In every letter, Vanda desperately asked about Demetrio, about how she could get in touch with him. In one letter, she wrote:

"I found out from Christo about your misfortune and the difficulties you are having during these tragic days of your life. I understand your pain and I sympathize with you. How desperately I want to be there to help you out of your darkness. Unfortunately we are so far from each other. Why my beloved, don't you write to me? Why don't you get in touch with me? At least I want to know that you are okay, that you are alive."

Demetrio listened carefully while Costa read out loud. When he finished with one letter, he reached for another. "This one here is the most recent," he said, and began skimming the pages silently. Demetrio saw Costa grimace. "My friend, I am now going to tell you something you are not going to like at all. Vanda has married."

"She got married?" Demetrio asked startled. "When did she get married?"

"Let me read the letter from the beginning."

Sao Paulo, Brazil

My Dearest Demetrio,

I hope this letter gets to you. All I ask is that before you judge me try to be fair. Our relationship was for me the most beautiful thing that could have happened in my life. With you I realized the meaning of true love. I am absolutely convinced that we were both sincere with each other. But life must go on. Suddenly I was left alone, without your companionship. I took solace in our child. This innocent little person gave me the courage to go on and hope for some kind of a future.

When I found out from your uncle Christo about the terrible blow that struck you, I went into shock. It was as if this misfortune had happened to my own family. I confess that I expected that at any moment the phone would ring and I would hear your voice. Honestly, I wanted so much to talk with you, to tell you that you are not alone in this world. That Costaki and I are here and are waiting for you. Unfortunately, the phone remained silent and my efforts to locate you through Christo and Costa proved fruitless. Nobody knew anything about you.

A few months ago, I met a man. He is also Greek, and his name is Yerasimo. We met at the Greek Orthodox Church where I go often. In the beginning, we were just friends, nothing else. Gradually, I started to like him. He is a wonderful young man from a good family. His parents own a big supermarket where he also works. From the very beginning, Yerasimo was very proper with me and showed me he had only good intentions towards me. When I went to the supermarket to shop, and naturally to see Yerasimo, he would stop whatever he was doing and devote his attention to Costaki. He would take him in his arms and play with him as if he was his own child. "My boy, Costaki," he would say and kiss him all over. Then he would put him in a shopping cart and give him rides in the aisles offering him lots of cookies, chocolates, and candy as well as many toys. Yerasimo's parents adore Costaki also. From the beginning Yerasimo has known all about my past and about the relationship I had with you. I did not hide anything from him. I decided to marry him because I believe that our child needs to be with a father, and I am certain he has found one. In a while, Costaki will go to school. Children who have no father are teased by other children. Before accepting Yerasimo's marriage proposal, I went to church and confessed because, if you remember, when we separated in Las Vegas, I swore on the golden cross you gave me for our child that he would never have another father but you. Do you remember it? The priest forgave me and lifted my oath. I hope you forgive me also. I want to assure you that as our child grows up, he will know the truth about his real father. Yerasimo agrees about this also. Whenever you want to talk to us on the phone or you want to come here and visit, you are welcome. I promise you that when Costaki can travel by himself and we know where you are, I will send him so you can meet him.

I end my letter now. I wish with all my heart that you are well and that you find the right path in your life, with God's help. I will never forget you, no matter how many years pass. You are a beautiful part of my life, and Costaki and I send you our greetings, kisses, and love.

Vanda & Costaki

P.S. Our wedding will be on Sunday, May 14. For now we will reside at my parents' house. You can call whenever you wish.

Costa translated the letter slowly, as Demetrio listened and Cathy looked on. Though she didn't understand what Costa was saying, she was certain, from Demetrio's expression, that it was unpleasant. When Costa had translated all the letters, Demetrio and Cathy thanked him for his help and said good-bye to him. As soon as they were in the car, Cathy asked him, "What's going on Demetrio, is there bad news?"

"Koukla, let's go home first. I want to talk to you."

Cathy looked at him silently, her apprehension growing. As soon as they were in their apartment, Demetrio went up to Cathy and hugged her. "Koukla, would you like to know what was in those letters?"

Cathy nodded.

"Vanda got married."

Cathy's face was so close to Demetrio's that they were separated only by a breath.

"Yes, Cathy, Vanda got tired of waiting for me. But Cathy, I love you, and every day that goes by I love you even more. And now I am free. Koukla, would you like to have me as your companion? Do you want to join the rest of our lives together?"

Cathy fell suddenly in his arms, crying.

"Princess, are you happy?"

"Demetrio, my heart is bursting. I never expected this. I want to be with you as long as God allows me to live." Then she looked up at him, and whispered, "Demetrio, I am pregnant."

It was Demetrio's turn to look at Cathy in joyous disbelief. "Koukla, my love, are you sure?"

"Yes, I am absolutely sure."

"And you tell me this so suddenly? Don't you know that my heart is not prepared for this kind of a shock?"

"I love you, Demetrio. I love you so much, like nothing else in the world."

"I love you too and I adore you, my princess. Now let's slowly get ourselves ready for our dinner. Today is a very special day for us."

The following day, Demetrio and Cathy sat down to discuss their future plans. "Koukla, where do you want us to live?"

"Demetrio, I can live anywhere in the world as long as I am with you. How does Salt Lake City sound to you? Did you like it, or do you prefer to go back to Greece?"

Demetrio smiled. "Now that I know what a beautiful place Salt Lake City is, I will go to my country only as a tourist during the summer time. Salt Lake will be a wonderful place to live."

"Demetrio, we can live in my parents' home for a while until we find our own. It's a large house, and my parents will be very pleased to have us with them."

"We have no idea yet what kind of jobs we can get," commented Demetrio.

"As long as we stay in my house, our expenses will be very low. I also have some savings in the bank where my father works. When I was born, he opened an account in my name and every month he deposits money in it. He always intended it to help me in the first months of my marriage. And now, that's about to happen," she said. "I am about to marry the prince of my dreams."

"I also have some savings in the bank," Demetrio said. "Before we leave, we can stop by there and I'll withdraw it all. I also have the gold Rolex watch I got as a gift from Nicholas. We can sell it. Oh yes, and I forgot to tell you something else," Demetrio said, pulling out of his wallet his uncle's check.

"Demetrio, what kind of money is that, darling? Ten thousand dollars! Where did you get that money?"

"It's a gift from my uncle."

"You know what I am thinking, Demetrio?"

"Say it."

"We can open up a store in Salt Lake City. My parents will help us, too."

"What kind of a store?" asked Demetrio.

"I don't know right now. When we get there, we can think about it and decide later. Demetrio, what do you think, should I call my parents and announce our news?"

"Koukla, do you have any doubt about my love for you or about my desire to have you as my wife for the rest of my life?"

"No, Demetrio, I don't have any doubt. But something scares me. I see so many good things happening to me that it is hard to believe this is real life and not a dream. This joy is too great to fit inside my heart. I am very thankful to you, Demetrio, for making me feel so much love for life."

"Koukla, I must be thankful to God forever for bringing you to me. You pulled me away from despair. If you had not helped me, I am sure I would be an alcoholic, probably just another drifter wandering the streets of L.A. Cathy, before you call your parents, I want us to go down to the West Side Pavilion. I have a surprise for you. We can walk there. I like to walk with you," said Demetrio as he kissed her.

When they arrived at the mall, Demetrio led Cathy to a jewelry store. "Oh Demetrio, darling, not now," Cathy protested. "Let's wait until we have more money."

But Demetrio put his arm around her waist, and coaxed her inside. "Koukla, I love you. That's all I have to say. I proposed to you and now I want to make it official. That is all."

Cathy fell again in his arms. "Demetrio, my darling, I will do everything within my power to see that you are always happy."

"But I am happy. I hope you can see that in my eyes."

An older woman with gray hair and glasses stood behind the jewelry counter. "How can I help you?" she asked.

"I want something to seal my engagement," said Demetrio.

She laughed. "You mean you want an engagement ring."

Demetrio looked at Cathy for a moment. "Is that what they call it, darling?"

Cathy nodded, trying to suppress her laughter.

"Yes, that's what I want," Demetrio replied.

The woman brought out a velvet-lined tray, and placed three diamond rings on it. Cathy looked at the prices, and drew Demetrio aside. "Demetrio, do you love me?" she asked looking in his eyes.

"Very much, my princess."

"Then, please listen to me. The diamond rings costing three and four thousand dollars are for those who have lots of money and don't know what to do with it. For me, it doesn't matter if the ring has diamonds. Demetrio, do you want to see me happy?"

"Always."

"Then, please let me choose the ring that I like."

Demetrio threw up his hands. "Whatever you want Koukla," he said.

Cathy looked through the display cases until a modest gold ring with an amethyst caught her eye.

"When is the lucky day?" the sales woman asked as she placed the ring in a jewelry box and rang up the sale.

"Very soon," replied Demetrio happily. "Very, very soon."

"You are a lucky man," the woman said. "So many women come in here and choose the most expensive ring – as if that matters. I wish you both a very long and happy life together."

When they were out of the store, Demetrio placed the ring on Cathy's finger. Cathy kept admiring and kissing it all the way home. "You kiss it, too, sweetheart," she asked Demetrio. "For good luck."

When they got home, Cathy called her parents. They talked for a long time, and Cathy promised that she and Demetrio would be home soon. Then she handed the phone to Demetrio so that he could talk with her father.

"How are you, Robert? As Cathy explained, in a few days we will be there with you."

"You are very welcome, Demetrio. Our house is always open to you."

"I have to come there, no matter what," said Demetrio. "I've got to beat you in at least one game of chess."

Robert's laughter boomed across the line. "Well hurry up and get safely here, and we'll see about the chess game," he said.

"Okay, Robert, we'll talk again when we get there."

"Very good Demetrio. Good-bye now. I'll be waiting for you."

"Cathy," Demetrio said when she hung up the phone. "I must make one phone call to Vanda."

"Call her, Demetrio. You owe her an explanation. I'll just go downstairs and clean out the car."

"Cathy, please stay. I want you to stay here when I talk with Vanda. I have no secrets to keep from you. You can talk to her yourself if you like to."

"No, Demetrio. Only you should talk to her."

When Cathy had gone, Demetrio dialed Vanda's number. A man quickly answered.

"Mr. da Silva?"

"Yes, this is he. Who is calling?"

"It's me, Demetrio. How are you, Mr. da Silva?"

"Is it you Demetrio? We are all okay. How are you? Where are you calling from?"

"From Los Angeles."

"How are you, son? How are things there? Why didn't you call us for such a long time? Are you okay, Demetrio?"

"Yes, I am okay. Thank you."

"Talk now with my daughter. She is right here. Bye from me. I am pleased that you are okay."

"Bye, Mr. da Silva, and thank for your kind words."

Suddenly Vanda was on the line. "Demetrio?"

"Hi, Vanda. How are you doing, how is Costaki?"

"We are all fine. Just tell me about yourself. Where are you, where have you been for such a long time? You were lost from the face of the earth."

"Vanda, I'm so sorry. Let me try to explain. When I lost my family, I went out of my mind. I didn't have the strength to deal with anything. For a long time I wandered around Los Angeles, drunk, lost. Many times I didn't recognize myself. I lost touch with reality."

Demetrio heard Vanda crying. "Poor Demetrio," she whispered. "How much you have suffered!"

Demetrio could no longer hold back his tears. After a few

moments, he spoke again. "Vanda, don't cry, my girl. Don't cry, because that makes me feel worse, too. I got your letters from Costa and found out that you were married. I understand perfectly, believe me, and I am very happy for you. And I, too, have met a nice woman. Her name is Cathy. I met her when I was wandering the streets drunk, lost in the dark alleys of loneliness and misery. This woman, Vanda, saved me. She helped me come out of my stupor. If our paths had not crossed, I surely would have died. When I got better, I talked to her about you and our child. I explained to her from the beginning that I belonged to you. Cathy accepted this and never tried to separate me from you, not even once. On the contrary, she tried with all her might to help me get my strength back and bring me back to life. My stay here in Los Angeles was like a nightmare for me. Even the word 'Los Angeles' reminded me of the tragedy I had been through. That's why we decided to go to Utah where Cathy's parents live so I could get away from the environment that reminded me of such sad things. Slowly, a kind of love developed between us, which gradually grew stronger and stronger. Nevertheless, when we returned back to Los Angeles, I started planning my trip to Brazil. I wanted to come to you because I knew you loved me and still wanted me. But I have to admit I had some doubts, because now I was in love with Cathy. When Costa read the letters to me and I found out that you were married, I accepted it. Now Cathy and I have decided to get married as well. What do you think about all these things, Vanda?"

"What can I say, Demetrio? I think everything is fine. Now that I know you are taken care of, I feel better. I am also relieved from the heavy burden that I carried with me, and I hope you live happily."

"Thank you, my little Vanda. I also wish you, from the bottom of my heart, to be always happy. Only don't forget to send me occasionally a picture of our son. When I settle down, I will send my address so you know where to find me."

"Okay Demetrio, I promise I will send you many photographs, and when Costaki is old enough to travel by himself, I will send him to you so you get to know each other."

"Thank you, Vanda. I will always have a corner of my heart devoted to you."

"Me too, Demetrio, I will never forget you."

"Bye Vanda, and good luck to you."

"Bye Demetrio. Good luck to you, too, my darling."

The following day, Cathy and Demetrio went to say hello to Lena, and to tell her the good news about the engagement.

"You picked a handsome man," Lena said when the two of them were left alone.

"Besides his good looks he has many other virtues," replied Cathy with a sly smile.

That same day Demetrio closed his bank account, sold his pick up truck, and he and Cathy began packing all her things so they could send the boxes with a moving company to Salt Lake City. A few days later, they set out in Cathy's car for her parent's home, some 650 miles away.

"You know, Demetrio," Cathy said with a playful smile, "Utah is full of Mormons, and in the old days Mormon men could take up to four wives – some still do. I hope you don't get bitten by the polygamy bug."

Immediately Demetrio's thoughts flew to Olga. "I have to figure out how to forget her," he thought to himself. "Cathy, I am a Greek Orthodox. My religion permits only one wife."

One month later, on a sunny Sunday, Demetrio and Cathy were married with family friends attending. For their honeymoon, they returned to Bardstown for another magical ride on the Old Kentucky Dinner train. Then they escaped to Hawaii for 15 blissful days. A few months later, their first child, a beautiful little girl, was born. They christened her Patricia. Patricia completed their happiness and brought joy to Cathy's parents.

A while later, with the help of Cathy's father, they opened a children's toy store on Main Street, the most central street in Salt Lake City. The large colored sign that was over the entrance read "THE GOLDEN HORSE." Demetrio and Cathy chose this name to always remember how they met each other.

Christo could no longer stand the loneliness and sold his house in Brentwood, placed all his real estate holdings with a management company, and moved permanently into a suite at the most glamorous casino in Las Vegas. During the summertime, when the temperature would break 120 degrees Fahrenheit, Christo would travel to Utah to spend several days with Demetrio's family.

In one of these trips, Christo met Leslie, a friend of Cathy's mother who had recently lost her husband. By now Christo was tired of being lonely and spending his nights with paid escorts. He proposed to Leslie, and she accepted. Christo left Las Vegas and moved to Salt Lake City for good.

Far away in Brazil, Vanda and Yerasimo also had a baby girl. Vanda wrote to Demetrio often, sending him photographs of his growing son and reminding him of her promise to send Costaki for a visit to America. During the summertime, Demetrio would take his family to Konitsa, and oftentimes Christo and Leslie would join them. Cathy was enchanted by the village. She fell in love with the people, who were so friendly and fun loving, and with the green forests and crystal clear waters of the Aoos River, where she and Demetrio would take their daughter swimming, and where they could all be happy and carefree. Then, when the summer began to fade, they would return to their home in Salt Lake City, where they lived their lives, happily.

SELECTED POEMS

CONSTANTIN CORALIS' ANTHOLOGY

Translated by Aristotle Michopoulos

America

America, America; you, friends and foes like to slander
when they get a chance. You, they want to blame,
but the truth is plain:
You help the whole world, when in danger of going under.

When any country is on the skids
you are the first to give a hand.
you are the giant with a child's heart
everyone you love, like a mother all her kids.

At quakes, tornados, floods or fiery heat,
you are always present.
and even those who don't like your presence
when in need, they kiss your feet.

You don't hold any grudges; you showed that in the past
even your enemies you help, when you can.
Your generocity is known to every man.
May the Lord keep you well, for the good of the world, at last!

Melissa

I met you when you were a little lass
And I was then a very young lad
Our homes were next to each other
To see you every day I wanted and no other

Your name was Melissa. I remember that well.
Our life was carefree; we were children then.
I promised you when I left my home
That on my return we'll make our own.

The big cities I visited, the dark streets I traversed
But in all my travels empty people I met.

Our village was full of trees and beautiful birds I would see
I still remember the children with laughter and glee.
The yard of my house was always in bloom
And we would weave dreams by the light of the moon.
My promise, Melissa, I was unable to keep
I'm lost far away, restless in my sleep.
And you, my house, and the neighborhood
I see now only in my dreamy mood.

The big cities I visited, the dark streets I traversed
But in àll my travels empty people I met.

Mother Nature

Mother nature can do nothing else.
She got tired of telling her children: "No more, no more!
Have Mercy! Don't destroy my environment any more.
Look around and you'll see everything grand is now in a mess."

In the name of progress and evolution you destroyed all:
Lakes, rivers, seas. You turned everything to black.
Our Planet is unique; there is still some life with some luck.
This perchance is our last chance. Restore its life of the yore.

Let everybody pitch in to this great effort.
Get involved; don't take such an apathetic stand.
Take a shovel, a hoe, a pickax in your hand
And turn our land to its former form.

No more factory or oil refinery.
No more cars spewing out their poisonous air.
Our lungs can no longer tolerate this affair.
Let's start this salvation task, before the end of our century.

Telephone and Umbrella

What are you looking for, my friend, in the darkness of the space?
Can't you really see that all is empty outside our domain?
Do you really wish to abandon our pretty plain?
I can assure you, you will never find such a great place.

Cast a glance around, look yonder.
You will see rivers, seas, flowers, birds and plants.
Cast a glance down to the sacred lands.
What a miracle, indeed, that they still feed the entire world.

For years now with your spaceships you travel, full of furor.
You talk about progress, hi-tech, and other exotic lace.
What's the use? The planet has become a terrible place.
The rich got richer and the poor are now poorer.

Everybody knows your obsessive fervor.
You want to discover till now unknown galaxies.
Years now you persist and you are full of fantasies.
To all this, I have only this to say: to me the top invention
so far has been the telephone and the umbrella.

The Pain

How do you measure pain?
What's the pain of a leper, all alone?
What's the pain of a mother, losing a child of her own?
What's the pain of the drunkard, whom a lost love
turned into a bum in vain?

How do you measure pain?
How sharp do you feel the pain, when you lose your own
and are left there sole?
How do you measure the pain of the soul?
What is really the pain of an orphan swain?

How do you measure pain?
What is the pain of the wounded in a battle,
who alone feels the loss?
How can you measure Christ's pain on the Cross?
How mach indeed he suffered dying, when they didn't
give him even a drop of water plain?

The Statue of Liberty

America, beloved country of my own
your fame the world over is very well-known.
Such strong magnets your wings they are
that draw the world from near and far.

The hungry, the persecuted, the oppressed of the world
only one hope for them remains firm;
to step foot on your hospitable soil they desire
the only path to survival: to that they aspire.

The peace of the world hangs from your hands
you demonstrate to all for what justice stands.
Loyal to your friends you are
ruthless to your foes by far.

America, from God you are blessed
and are protected and protect the rest.
Across the land blows the air of democracy
with its ever-wakeful guardian –the Statue of Liberty.